T0117485

NO TIME TO
Regret

PREVIOUSLY PUBLISHED BOOKS

Reading Problems, by Margaret Ann Richek,
Lynne List, and Janet W. Lerner

Music, Art, & Drama Experiences for the Elementary Curriculum

NO TIME TO
Regret

LYNNE LIST

WESTBOW
PRESS®
A DIVISION OF THOMAS NELSON
& ZONDERVAN

Archway Publishing books may be ordered through booksellers or by contacting:

Archway Publishing
1663 Liberty Drive
Bloomington, IN 47403
www.archwaypublishing.com
844-669-3957

ISBN: 978-1-4808-9884-4 (sc)
ISBN: 978-1-4808-9885-1 (hc)
ISBN: 978-1-4808-9886-8 (e)

Library of Congress Control Number: 2020921466

Print information available on the last page.

Archway Publishing rev. date: 12/28/2020

This book is dedicated to my mother and
father, who always had confidence in me
and encouraged me in all things in life.

Introduction

This is a compelling story of an illicit love affair that comes back to haunt those involved years later. When it rears its ugly head, it stirs up memories and events that will affect the lives of six people. The story brings a highly emotional and unusual human problem to the forefront. Bob Ruthers is faced with the most difficult task of his life—he must make a challenging moral decision.

 *Est modus in rebus.*

There is moderation in all things.

Prologue

It was in Greeben, South Carolina, on January 12, 1943, that Allison Bishop, in a state of semiconsciousness, was vaguely aware of her hands being tied at her sides and her legs bound, one to the extreme right and the other to the left, to what seemed to be two large rings suspended from somewhere above her. She bore down in a final desperate attempt to rid her body of the child and recognized the sweet, sickening smell of ether filter through her nostrils and into the depths of her lungs.

Fall asleep! Fall asleep! she commanded herself as she felt the doctor's fingers working nimbly at a part of her body that now seemed far away and completely detached from the remainder of her being. Then she saw the circles of red, yellow, green, and blue spinning before her face, and she knew unconsciousness was about to overtake her.

Thank God! she thought as the rippling rings spun by faster and faster, contracting and releasing, enlarging and closing like a mouth uttering silent words as they whirled about. Gradually, their utterings became audible and then louder and louder until the words rang harshly in her ears.

"Bas—tard? Your–child? Bas—tard? Your–child? Bastard? Your child?" they asked over and over again, increasing the rapidity of their words as they did so.

"Forgive me," she pleaded to the flaming mouths. "Forgive me, I don't know."

"Bas—tard? Bas—tard? Bas—tard?" they continued to question in mocking tones.

She reached out in a vain attempt to grab one of the rings, missing it as it danced quickly between her fingers. It beckoned to the others and, leaving their brilliant circles, they broke into thousands of pieces. Then, like a kaleidoscope making multiple intricate patterns, they followed their leader into brilliant designs.

Suddenly, she was standing at trial alongside a dozen red jurors. Before her sat the blue judge with a yellow stenographer writing rapidly at his side.

The green clerk swore her in. "Do you swear to tell the truth, the whole truth, and nothing but the truth, so help you God?" he asked sternly.

"I do," she answered quietly.

"What is your name?" Boomed the judge.

"Allison Bishop."

"Nee what?" he asked.

"Allison Zell."

"Your husband is?"

"George Bishop."

"You're married for how long?" he asked curtly.

"Ten months."

"Was there not another you knew as intimately as George?"

"Yes." She hung her head in remorse.

"His name?"

"Robert."

"His full name?" he questioned.

"Robert Ruthers." Her answers were softly spoken and barely audible.

"Did you know him before your husband?"

"Yes."

"Did you know him after?"

"Yes." Her reply was quietly pitiful.

"Who fathered your child?"

"I don't know."

"Red jury," he began, turning toward them, "how do you find this woman?"

"Guilty, guilty, guilty, guilty," they chanted gleefully as they joined forces once again and spun in a circle of delight.

"Let me explain!" she screamed over the commotion.

"Guilty, guilty, guilty," the chant continued.

"Allison Bishop," the blue judge roared, ignoring her plea. "We hereby find you guilty of producing what may be a bastard child, and we condemn you to a life of doubt."

"Wait!" she cried.

"Of doubt! Of doubt! Of doubt!" he yelled.

The courtroom disappeared, and the circles returned. They spun endlessly, quietly, drifting farther and farther from her until they were but a speck in the distance. Then they were gone.

Her stomach felt odd, like it did when she was in an elevator.

"You had a boy—eight pounds, one ounce," the nurse said, and then she repeated it since Allison was still not quite out of the anesthesia or fully aware.

"A son?" Allison whispered.

"Yes."

"Raymond Ryan," she sighed aloud, and then she sank slowly into an undisturbed sleep.

Chapter 1

JULY 1969

The days of the summer on Long Island were invariably damp and hot, but the humidity of the afternoons was habitually compensated for with a delightfully cool ocean breeze in the evenings. Thus was the climate of the south shore, the north being forced to resort to the bay for any and all relief.

Robert Ruthers, called Bob by his friends, resided on the southernmost tip of the island, just five miles from Atlantic Beach. He had been living in the town of Woodmere for six years and had become so much a part of this community that he no longer thought of or remembered Brooklyn as being his home. His fine, white clapboard, two-story colonial house was one of eight homes on the curving, dead-end Ivy Lane. The residence was quite impressive to the eye. Black shutters curtained every front window, and large pillars rose from their bases on the stone entrance porch to the second floor, where they supported a small wooden terrace railed in white. Surrounding the house on all sides were shrubs and flowers carefully planned by the gardener so that something would be in bloom throughout three fruitful seasons. The border before the façade boasted innumerable azalea, hydrangea, and rhododendron bushes, which were chosen for their position of honor because they remained green year-round.

"You can't have dead, brown shrubs in the front all winter, Mr. Ruthers," the gardener had maintained when Bob first bought the house. "That would look terrible."

Bob had agreed. He realized then that there was much to be learned about maintaining a home properly.

"Where I come from," Bob had replied, "we were fortunate if we had enough dirt to plant a bush without worrying about what we were planting."

The life Bob was leading was completely foreign to what he had known previously. There had been years of struggling just to get by, a succession of moves from apartment to apartment, then a move from a two-family house to an attached home of his own in Brooklyn, and finally to Woodmere. Each step had been a slight improvement upon the last. And with each he never lost sight of his ultimate goal.

It took thirteen years for his dream to materialize. Long Island was the symbol of his prosperity. Some men feel success when they can afford a mink coat for their wives, a boat for themselves, or a Cadillac for their families. Bob dreamed of none of these, only of a fine home in a wealthy community, surrounded by people who mattered, who could help him make a better life—the best life—for him, his wife, and most of all his daughter.

Lorene was twelve years old when she made her home in Ivy Lane. She had already attended four different public schools and was apprehensive about her enrollment into the fifth since her father had stressed that she was about to meet fine, intelligent people. In addition, she hated the idea of leaving a school with departmentalized classes to one where she had to remain in the same classroom all day. She had no choice, but she disliked school from that point forward.

Bob wasn't a snob, intellectually or financially. He merely wanted the most that he could get and was willing to settle for no less. This July evening he was resting in a contour lounge on the screened-in terrace, thinking idly of his climb from a straight-back chair on the fire escape of a dingy, hot apartment to an attached two-story house in Brooklyn and then to the cool ocean breeze on a porch in Woodmere. He was a fine-looking man for his age. Aristocratically gray at the temples, he was still in possession of the rest of his wavy black hair. His waist had taken on a middle-aged spread, but the remainder of his physique was muscular and slender enough that he could not be considered excessively heavy.

Lorene sat opposite him, her head buried in the evening paper, and he gazed at his daughter in silent admiration. At eighteen, she had lost the child-like characteristics he remembered and loved so dearly. She was a young woman now, blossoming into full maturity but still exhibiting the radiant face and expressions permitted only to the young. Gone were the clumsy antics of the chubby child, the total dependence upon adult decisions, the youthful innocence of the face and body. He loved the child then, and he loved the woman now. It amazed him that they were one and the same.

Looking at Lorene, he marveled at how attractive she was. Her slim, well-formed figure crowned with shining black hair; her red bud-like lips so kissable at a glance; her perceptive brown eyes reflecting a sensitive, understanding soul—this was his daughter, and there was nothing in the universe too good for her.

Lorene put aside the daily crossword puzzle and looked at her dad.

"Either I'm getting too smart or these puzzles are getting easier," she said. "I've finished it already."

"The puzzles are getting easier," Bob teased. "There's no doubt of that."

"Thank ye for thy compliment, Sir Tease," Lorene replied

with a gallantly sweeping gesture. "And with that final retort, I shall retire to my boudoir lest the fleeting moments deprive me of adequate time to adorn myself for my oncoming appointment."

"Off on another date tonight, Princess?"

"Yup! Joyce wangled a blind date with a friend of her fiancé. You've met Alan Rice, haven't you, Dad?"

"I think so." He looked pensive for a moment until the recollection was revived. "He's that short, blond-haired boy studying engineering, isn't he? I think I remarked on what a nice-looking couple they made."

"Correct on both counts," Lorene answered. "Well, this fellow is his roommate at school. He's entering his senior year too. He's a little older. He was in the army before he started college."

"Well, that's nice going for a lower classman, isn't it?" he teased again.

"I refuse to answer that question on the grounds that you are mocking me again," she replied.

"Who's teasing whom?" Gloria Ruthers asked as she entered the porch carrying a large platter of fruits. "As if I didn't already know."

The resemblance between mother and daughter was remarkable. Face to face, the two women were likened unto a mirror of time reflecting the portrait of youth on one side counterbalanced by twenty additional years of maturity on the other. Yet, side by side, they had been mistaken for sisters since Gloria was still very youthful looking.

"And just *how* are you teasing your daughter now, Bob?" Gloria asked. After many years of marriage, she had accustomed herself to the teasing, which she considered an irritating characteristic. But she accepted it, secretly hoping that someday he would outgrow it.

"Just having some fun, sweetheart," he answered. "Lorene doesn't mind, do you, honey?"

"Not really, Dad. I love you too much." She moved to his chair and placed a kiss on his right cheek. "And understand you too well," she added. "Now I had better get started."

"Before you go, young lady," Gloria interrupted, "how about giving your mother a chance at the paper. Where is it?"

"On the end table next to the chaise!" Lorene shouted as she raced through the hall and up the stairs.

As he followed the sound of her footsteps until they disappeared somewhere on the second floor, Bob thought about what a lucky man he was, realizing that no man could ask for more.

❧

"Does that sound all right to you, Bob?" Gloria asked.

"What was that again?" He hadn't listened to her question. "I'm afraid I didn't hear you."

"I asked if you wanted to go to a movie tonight."

"Oh, I don't think so. You know how I feel about the movies—the fewer the better for me."

"But we haven't gone in so long, and there's an excellent picture playing."

"Why not call up Gladys and Ed?" he suggested. "If they're not doing anything, maybe we'll play some bridge tonight."

"Then you definitely don't want to see a show?" she asked, a bit disappointed.

"No, not tonight."

"All right." She folded the paper carefully and placed it on the end table. "What were you thinking of before? You were so far away."

"Nothing special."

"You were certainly absorbed."

"It wasn't anything. Only what a very lucky man I am. What time is it now?"

Gloria looked at her watch. It was small and neat with a cluster of diamonds at either end of the dial. It had been a birthday present from Bob.

"Seven thirty," she said, "but its accuracy depends on how good a gift you gave me," she joked. Gloria figured that if he could tease, so could she.

"I would only give you the best," he answered seriously. "But then, I'm sure you know that."

"Of course," she answered, and then added, "What time is Lorene's date coming?"

"Not sure. I think about eight thirty. Why?"

"No special reason. Just wondered. What's this fellow's name?"

"I don't know. He's a blind date," Bob said." "Lorene told me he is a roommate of Joyce's fiancé."

Gloria suddenly remembered. "Come to think of it, I think she told me his name is Raymond. She joked about him being called Ray. She thought that was funny. She said it made her think of sunshine. She also told me that he has a middle name, and he always uses it. So he's Raymond Ryan. She thought that was funny too. Why would a young man always use his first and middle name? According to Joyce, though, he's a very nice boy." Gloria did not notice the sudden change of expression on Bob's face when she mentioned the name Raymond Ryan. She was thumbing through the paper as she spoke to him.

Bob was shocked. He sat, looking at nothing and mouthing the name, "Raymond Ryan."

"That's right, dear. It's a nice name, isn't it? Kind of elegant, right?"

Bob heard none of the questions. He was deep in thought.

"I said, it's a nice name, isn't it?"

"Yes, very nice," he answered matter-of-factly.

"Whatever is the matter? You look sort of pale. And you're far away somewhere, not even hearing what I'm saying." She put the newspaper down and stared at him.

"I'll be all right, just a pang of indigestion," he lied.

"Shall I get you something?" she asked solicitously.

"I said I'd be all right," he replied. He was not able to get the name Raymond Ryan from his mind.

"Do you want me to call Gladys and Ed now about the bridge game, or would you rather stay home?"

"No, no, You call them. I'd like to play bridge tonight," he answered, though he really didn't want to. But he thought it might take his mind off of Raymond Ryan.

As Gloria went to the telephone, Bob tried to dismiss the idea from his mind. *It's just a coincidence*, he reassured himself. *After all, there must be more than one Raymond Ryan in the world. Or perhaps Gloria made a mistake. It's possible she was in error about the name. It could be Raymond Robert, or Raymond Randy, or Raymond Ralph. It could be a million different possibilities. Yet,* he thought, *the boy would be about twenty-five or -six now. If he spent a few years in the army, he could possibly be a senior in college now.* He sat erect and shaking his head in an effort to rid himself of his thoughts. He asked himself, *What am I thinking? I must stop. It can't be the same boy. It isn't. It's just a mistake. I left my past behind years ago. It can't come back to haunt me now.*

"Gladys and Ed would love to play bridge tonight, honey. I told them we'd be there about nine o'clock. Is that okay with you?" Gloria asked as she reentered the room. She waited a minute for a response. "Is that okay with you, Bob? "she repeated. "Whatever is the matter with you tonight? You are so preoccupied."

He hadn't heard her enter, but he sensed her presence when she was repeating her question.

"Nothing is the matter," he replied. "Nothing at all. Yes, that's fine with me."

"We should have a nice evening," she said. "They're good bridge players. Now, promise me you won't overbid, like you have a tendency to do."

"I promise, Gloria. And yes, it should be a lovely evening."

Bob was aware of everything Gloria said, but his mind was off in a different direction. He was worried. If Raymond Ryan was who he thought he was, what would this mean for his life? For his daughter's life? And, most important, what would this mean for his marriage? After all these years, he was certain his past was long since gone.

Chapter 2

At exactly 8:30 p.m. the doorbell rang, and Bob, knowing who it was as he walked to the entrance, opened the door slowly and systematically scanned the countenance of the strange boy standing before him. It was a nice face, manly and pleasant with a shock of brown wavy hair falling carelessly atop a wide brow that edged two small, twinkling, blue eyes. A Roman nose and a broad white smile completed the bronzed face, and despite his instinct to dislike the boy, Bob had to admit that he was extremely likable. He was dressed in sport clothes—navy blue slacks, a white shirt closed at the neck with a navy and gray polka-dot bow tie, and a gray linen sport jacket. His shoes were black and shined to a lustrous finish, a quality Bob had always looked for and admired in a man. His socks were of blue, gray, and red in an argyle pattern. All of this detail Bob observed in a minute.

"How do you do, sir," the boy said, extending his hand. "I have a date with Lorene tonight. My name is Raymond Ryan Bishop."

"Hello," Bob answered casually. His arm automatically reached out to grasp the boy's, but his mind was not on the handshake. Instead, he thought fleetingly, *There's no mistake. He looks exactly like his mother.* "I'm Lorene's father," he said. "Won't you come in?"

"Thank you, Mr. Ruthers." He stepped in and looked about. "Is Lorene ready?"

"She will be in a moment. Come into the living room and sit down."

"Thank you, sir. I hope she won't be long; the others are waiting in the car outside." He glanced around the room taking in the lovely décor. "This is a very nice house you have here," he said politely.

"Thank you," Bob replied.

They sat quietly, Ray not knowing just what to say to the father of a girl he did not know and Bob hesitating to ask the questions he longed to blurt out. The quiet was deadening.

"Can I offer you some candy, Raymond?" Bob asked, extending the candy dish on the cocktail table.

"No, thank you. And please call me Ray. I use my nickname all the time."

Bob had decided previously that he would have to make the most of the short time that he would have alone with the boy. It would be his only opportunity to attempt to find out, with certainty, if this was the same Raymond Ryan he had known of only briefly so many years before.

"Do you live around here, Ray? On Long Island, I mean?" he asked nonchalantly as though he was just making conversation.

"No, sir. I'm from Clinton, New Jersey."

Bob sighed in relief inwardly and relaxed. The boy he knew was from the South—South Carolina to be exact.

"But we weren't always from New Jersey, sir," Ray continued, forcing Bob to tighten up again. "We moved up here from Greeben, South Carolina, when I was four."

"Then you're actually from the South?" Bob prayed the anxiety in his voice was not noticeable.

"My mother is. My father was a Yankee but settled in the South after he and my mother were married. He got a good job up here, though, and so they moved. I don't consider myself a Southerner because I really don't remember living any place but in Jersey."

"And does your mother have one of those truly charming Southern names, like Mary Lou?" Bob asked. He was trying to seem politely inquisitive and as casual as he knew how. He hoped the boy wouldn't think his questioning excessive.

"No, not at all. Her name is Allison."

There was no longer reason for suspicion; all of Bob's doubts were confirmed. This was the same boy, but as he looked at him, it was difficult for him to believe.

"Ray?" Lorene said as she entered the room.

"You must be Lorene," he replied, standing. "I'm Ray Bishop."

"Hi! Where are Joyce and Alan?"

"They're waiting in the car. Are you ready now?"

"Yes, I am. Good night, Dad. Don't wait up. I might be late."

"Good night, honey," Bob answered absentmindedly. "Have a good time."

"Good night, Mr. Ruthers," Ray said, extending his hand once again. "It was nice meeting you."

Bob listened for the door to close and leaned back in his chair. This was all too much, like a bad dream from which he couldn't wake. *A weird coincidence that is most likely a one-in-a-million chance,* he thought. *But it happened. What can I do?*

He contemplated for a moment and then, trying to reassure himself, thought, *This is silly, plain foolishness. She'll go out with him a few times, and that will be that. He'll go back to school in September, they'll never see each other again, and they'll forget they ever knew each other. He's no different from the others she's gone out with, and she's tired of them quickly enough. Lord knows, Lorene has had her pick of the crop.* But then again, he thought doubtfully, *what if he's not just another date? What if … ?* He stood up, began pacing the floor, and tried to convince himself that he had to stop thinking that way. *Nothing will come of this. Nothing.*

"Are you ready to leave, Bob?" Gloria asked from the doorway. "I told Gladys that we'd be there at nine."

"I'm ready. Let's go."

They locked the door behind them and walked down the street toward Gladys's house. The street was deserted, and with just the moonlight and the lights from a few lampposts, there was an eerie feeling as they moved along in the darkness. But this was the charm of suburbia, and they had accustomed themselves to it. A stronger breeze had begun and was manipulating the leaves, making them dance in jerky movements like puppets on a string. The night was clear, and the full moon, surrounded by twinkling stars, filled the air with a quiet reminiscence of peace and serenity.

Bob picked up his step. *I'm the lucky one*, he thought. *Things always go right for me. Lorene will forget all about Raymond Ryan Bishop within two weeks. There's nothing to worry about.*

"Ready to play a good game of bridge tonight, honey?" he asked. "I'm really in the mood."

"Then you're feeling better?" she asked.

"Better? No, not better. I'm all well."

Chapter 3

Gladys and Ed Sykes had been occupying their English Tudor-style house at the end of Ivy Lane for ten years when Gloria and Bob migrated from Brooklyn. Consequently, being the friendly people that they were, they inaugurated their new neighbors into the wonders of suburban living. In a sense the area was almost rural since, just beyond their street and across a dirt road, there was a large farm where fresh vegetables could be purchased and a stable with horses where one could rent a horse and go riding.

"You'll love it here," Gladys had said when she dropped in for "just a minute" on their second day of nonurban living. "The people are wonderful. They take newcomers into their midst as if they had lived here all their lives. There's an excellent school system and clubs and organizations galore to keep you busy. Do you like doing charity work?" she had asked almost in the same breath.

Gloria had laughed in response and then said, "You sound like a walking advertisement."

"I guess I do." She thought for a moment. "But that's because I love it here so. You and your husband must come over for an evening," she continued. "Ed is anxious to meet you. Do you think you could make it this Friday?"

"My social calendar is completely empty at the moment, so Friday will be fine." Gloria replied.

From that time on it had been a whirlwind of introductions and invitations for the Ruthers until, in a matter of a few months, they had intricately woven themselves into their new life and their home was filled with the happiness and contentment for which they had so long been in search.

This evening Bob leaned back in his chair and surveyed his surroundings. He was the dummy in this hand and, realizing that their three no-trump bid was impossible to beat, he relaxed his attention to glance idly about.

Nothing had changed in the last six years since Gladys and Ed had added a den in the rear of the house, behind the kitchen. The knotty pine walls were stained in their natural color, the casement windows wore the same two-tiered black-and-white-plaid café curtains with large brass rings joining them to the wide brass rods. A salt-and-pepper early American couch, resting alongside a large bay window, was shown to advantage by two small marble-topped coffee tables standing before it. Directly opposite the pieces were two louvered folding doors guarding the entrance arch like stiff wooden soldiers at attention. To the right of the protectors was a gray armchair with a spinning wheel lamp table placed gingerly at its side. These two pieces stood alongside a large fireplace tiled with abstract decorative blocks. In the corner where the bridge game was being played, floor-to-ceiling built-in bookcases were on either side of an enormous picture window. The circular pine card table was surrounded by four straight-backed armchairs.

Bob noted that the room, as well as the people, were still the same. The years did not seem to have changed them at all. Ed sat to his right—grim faced now in his attempt to defeat the contract—but normally jolly, a credit to the adage pertaining to obese people. He was a dark-haired man, balding in the center, with a round, full face and a body to match. Gladys, on the other hand, was daintily built and weighed no more than one hundred and ten pounds, which was underweight for her five feet, five inches. Her hair, pulled back severely into a bun that rested on the nape of her neck, had begun to gray at the temple. The hairstyle plus the graying and the slight rings of age beneath her eyes indicated that the years were starting to take their toll. Her fingers drummed idly on the tabletop as an unconscious outlet for her nervous energy. Since Bob had known Gladys, she had displayed a tendency toward being extremely nervous and worrisome. As the years had gone by, this characteristic had become more pronounced, and today her tension was more obvious even while she was at play.

"Bid three and made six," Gloria said triumphantly. "How come you didn't keep the bidding open, Bob?"

"I knew we could make three; I wasn't sure of six," he replied. "And we didn't need any more since we were vulnerable anyway."

"Some bridge player you are!" she exclaimed. "Shall we play one more rubber?"

"We will if you want to," Gladys answered, "but it is getting rather late. I suggest we have our coffee and cake now."

Everyone agreed, and in a matter of minutes the table was set and the coffee being poured.

"I have something to tell you," Gladys announced when everyone had added their cream, stirred in their sugar, and relaxed with the first sip. "Ed and I are going to be grandparents."

"Oh, Gladys, how very wonderful for you!" Gloria answered enthusiastically. "You must be thrilled."

"I am. I don't know how I'll ever wait out the time."

"When is the baby due?" Bob asked casually. For some unexplained biological reason, men are never as enthusiastic over marriages and births as are women.

"In January sometime. She's going to the hospital right here in

Far Rockaway, and she's using a doctor from here too. No reason for her to travel into the city when the same accommodations are nearby." She was speaking about her daughter, although she could have meant her daughter-in-law, but Gloria knew that Gladys's son and his wife lived in another state.

"Of course not," Gloria said in response to Gladys's comment. "When you see Eileen, will you offer her our congratulations? And Pete too, of course."

"Certainly I will. I was dying to tell you sooner, but we wanted to wait a bit to be certain."

"What a grandmother she's going to be," Ed remarked. "Judging from her reaction now, she's bound to fuss every time the baby cries."

"I will not, Ed Sykes." She was indignant. "I certainly will not. I'm not going to be one of those interfering grandmothers, no more than I am a mother-in-law."

"But what a temptation with your grandchild only five minutes away," he joked.

"Now, you stop teasing me or Gloria and Bob will think I'm terrible. But don't forget we've waited five years for this grandchild."

"We know Ed's joking," Gloria assured her. "He's beginning to sound like Bob. It must be catching from long association." She reached over and patted Gladys's hand. "It's perfectly understandable how you feel. I have a daughter of my own, and I can't even imagine how I'll feel. Don't you let Ed get the best of you now."

Gladys smiled and looked over at Ed. "He's really more thrilled than I am, but he just won't admit it."

Ed ignored the remark. "You should see the letter the kids sent informing us of the happy event. My Eileen is a great one for writing, you know, and she said that they were so excited she didn't think she could express herself half as well in conversation as in a letter. She wrote the news on the inside of a birthday card to Gladys and told her she was to get the greatest gift of her life. What a letter!"

"Speaking of letters," Gladys interrupted, "and changing the subject, did you hear about Joe Peterson?"

Joe Peterson was the mailman for Ivy Lane and numerous streets surrounding it. He had been serving the area, without missing a day, for two years. He was a likeable fellow who had made friends with everyone on his route and stopped for a cup of coffee with some in the winter and lemonade with others in the summer. The neighborhood had gone through crises with him—a painful wisdom tooth, his wife's appendicitis attack, and the birth of a son. He was a young man, in his late twenties, and a source of joy to everyone who knew him for he truly loved his work and the people he met.

"No, I haven't heard a thing," Gloria confessed, a bit puzzled. "What happened?"

"It seems that he may be fired," Gladys said almost in a whisper as though she was repeating some gossip.

"Fired? From a civil service job? For what?" Bob asked.

Gladys answered quickly, "I don't know. I haven't had a chance to talk to him since I heard about it two days ago."

"It must be a mistake," Gloria said. "Just a rumor, or maybe someone misunderstood and he just said he wouldn't be delivering because he was going on vacation." She looked at her watch. "My goodness, just see the time. We'd better be going."

After the "good nights" and "congratulations again" were said, Gloria and Bob headed for home. Both were weary and anxious to get to sleep. They arrived home in a few minutes, went right to the bedroom, and quickly prepared for bed.

"Isn't it wonderful news about Eileen?" Gloria asked as she slid into bed alongside Bob.

"Uh-huh." His eyes were already closed, and he appeared half-asleep.

"I almost wish Lorene ..." she said dreamily, not finishing her sentence.

"She has plenty of time," Bob answered as he rolled over. "Plenty of time," he repeated. "Gosh," he added, "this is the most comfortable bed in the world. Good night, honey." He said it softly, throwing her a kiss at the same time. All thoughts of his early evening fears were dissipated in the exhaustion of his body.

Chapter 4

The air was saturated with exhaust fumes and the smell of burnt rubber as the two couples elbowed their way through the crowd toward the nearest exit at the Freeport Raceway. The last of the stock car races for the evening had reached its conclusion, and the swarms of departing people produced so great a din that one could hardly be audible over it. The lights focused on the track made the layers of blue-gray smoke hovering close to the ground eerily visible. Lorene put her hand to her face and felt a gritty covering of rubber dust on her skin. They had been sitting on the first turn, and the breeze had carried the black particles thrown from the skidding vehicles.

"I must look a mess!" Lorene exclaimed aloud, dismayed at the thought of her appearance.

"What did you say?" Ray asked as he cupped his hand about his ear in an effort to catch her words.

In a shout, she repeated her exclamation, and he replied, "We're all sort of messy. But let's go somewhere for a bite to eat and clean up there."

"That sounds fine," Lorene answered.

"Have you any suggestions?" he asked loudly. "I don't know anything at all about the island."

"Do you like pizza? I know of a nice place not far from here."
They had progressed past the ticket gate and were weaving their way between cars in the parking lot.

"I love it," Ray answered. "How about you two?

Joyce and Alan were walking directly in front of them and evidently had overheard the conversation for they replied rapidly.

"Whatever you want is okay with us. We're very agreeable this evening," Alan said, and with that Joyce squeezed his arm a bit tighter and leaned a little closer.

"Then pizza it is," Ray replied as they reached the car.

Joyce and Alan scrambled into the back seat of Ray's "pride and joy." The car was a blue-and-white Chevrolet four-door, hard-top model and possessed every extra that could be wanted. Ray knew that his parents were overextending themselves when they suggested buying it for him as a gift when he completed his term in the army. Though he had refused to consider accepting such a present, they had insisted, maintaining it was what they wanted him to have. He loved the car and had named it Shasta. "The reason," he explained, "is that 'shehasta' have gas, 'shehasta' have oil, 'shehasta' be washed, and so on." They all laughed.

A few minutes later, they were headed west on Sunrise Highway. Joyce and Alan, engaged in their own conversation of plans for their wedding, had left Lorene to flounder on her own. Making conversation had always been difficult for her, especially when she knew so little about the boy she was with. Though she could jabber on and on when she felt at ease and knew her escort well, words were hard to come by when she was conscious of attempting to make a good impression.

"I really enjoyed the races," she said after lighting a cigarette. "I'm so glad we went there, even though we were a bit late and didn't see the first race. I never realized what I was missing before. It's such fun and so exciting."

"I love them," Ray replied. "I go as often as I can. After a while you get to know the drivers and their cars, and it's much more interesting when you're following them." He spoke without looking at her. His eyes were intent on the road.

"I guess so," she mused. "How long have you been interested in cars?"

"Almost as long as I can remember. I was always mechanically inclined. That's why I want to be an engineer."

"Did you know that my dad is an engineer?' she asked.

"Really? Where does he work?"

"In New York. Oh, turn right at the next light. He works for a pneumatic conveying system company. It's interesting. He designed a cleaning system for airport runways. My mom named it the JARC for Jet Aircraft Runway Cleaner. Did you know that the engines of jets are so low they pick up everything on the runway?"

"I heard that. He must really know his stuff. Is your dad a mechanical engineer?" he asked as he rounded the corner.

"Uh-huh. You'd enjoy his workshop. He loves to do things around the house, and he's loaded with all the newest of everything. He boasts about how he used to be able to take a car apart and put it together again in the good old days before autos became a specialized field with individual tools needed for each make."

Ray laughed. "Your dad sounds interesting. Oh, is that the restaurant off to the right? Cairo's Italian Cuisine?"

"That's it."

He pulled into the lot, found an empty space, and parked.

"Hey, you two lovebirds in the back, we're here," he called over his shoulder. "But I promise not to turn around until you give the all clear."

"Rib us if you want," Alan replied, "but wait until you're engaged. He who laughs last, you know."

Once inside the restaurant the boys looked for a table while the girls headed for the washroom. They found that it was typical of the type of restroom one would expect in a small restaurant—dark and dirty.

"Well," Joyce asked expectantly as she reapplied her lipstick, "what do you think of him? He likes you."

"He's very nice," Lorene replied. She had just combed her hair and was waiting for Joyce to complete her finishing touches. She was surprised at Joyce's remark. "How do you know he likes me? What makes you say that?"

"Alan said he can tell. He's been out on dates with Ray before. He knows him very well."

"I guess I should be complimented."

"You should be," Joyce answered, waving the lipstick tube in the air as she talked. "Ray's one of the most sought-after fellows on the campus, and after all there are lots more fish in the sea at RPI for those Russell Sage girls to throw bait to. So I guess he must have something."

"He does," Lorene answered, "and I do think he's very nice."

"Well, you don't sound very enthusiastic about it. You know we had to go to a lot of trouble to get him to come tonight. He hates blind dates."

"Maybe I'm just not ready to meet someone," she answered.

"What do you mean, you're not ready?"

"Oh, nothing, I guess. Just that I'm having such a good time dating around. I'm not thinking about settling in with one person."

"Well, when the right one comes along, you'll change your mind."

Lorene led the way into the dining room. The place was small and picturesque. Red-and-white checkered cloths covered the tiny round tables, and wine bottles, encrusted with multicolored layers of wax, stood in their centers with thick candles glittering from their mouths. There were no other lights. The same fabric that appeared on the tables curtained the windows and was tightly drawn, leaving the room in almost complete darkness. A three-piece combo stood in one corner playing soft music while a few couples danced around the tiny dance floor.

The boys were waiting when Lorene and Joyce sat down at the table. They had just placed an order for a large pie with mushrooms and sausages.

"How about a drink?" Ray asked. "I'm having a beer."

"Me too," Joyce said.

"Make that three," Alan chimed in.

"Not me. I'll have a Coke," Lorene said. "I don't drink, and I hate beer.

"I'm hungry," Joyce said.

"I want to dance," Alan replied as he took her hand.

"How about you, Lorene?" Ray asked. "Would you care to dance?"

"I love dancing," she replied softly.

The band was playing a fox-trot as they reached the floor. It was an old melody that seemed vaguely familiar to Lorene. She thought it must have been popular when she was about five or six years old. For a few minutes she hummed the melody, and then the title came to mind. The song had been remade a number of times since its inception.

"'You've Gotta Have Heart'—isn't that the name of the song?" she asked Ray.

"I think so. It sounds sort of familiar. I can't do it justice, though, for I'm really not much of a dancer," Ray apologized. "I just can't seem to get my feet to do what I want them to."

"I think you're doing beautifully," she answered, and she really meant it.

They danced on quietly for a few minutes until Ray broke the silence.

"Have you ever seen the midget races?" he asked.

"No. Are they different from the stocks we saw tonight?"

"Completely. The cars are different, smaller and no tops. They race on Friday nights. Would you like to go with me next Friday?"

"Yes, I would," Lorene answered and then added, "very much."

"I have a sort of tentative appointment, but I can break it easily," he said.

"Are you sure you want to do that? We can make it some other Friday."

"I don't mind. Besides, next Friday brings us into August, and that only leaves me one month or so before I head back to Troy and school. I'd like to take you out a few times so that you can really appreciate the races," he added. That wasn't his real reason, but he hesitated to say what he really wanted.

"Look, the waiter is bringing our pizza. We'd better go back to the table."

When the pie was consumed, along with the beer and Coke, the hour was late so they started for home. The night was lovely and clear, and as they drove Lorene and Ray spoke more easily and learned a good bit about each other.

"You're a remarkable girl, Lorene," Ray said. "I'm glad Alan fixed up this date."

"You're pretty remarkable yourself," she replied. "It's amazing how alike we are in so many ways."

"If you two don't cut out the flattery, you'll be driving right past Joyce's house," Alan's voice bellowed from the rear.

"I can take a hint," Ray laughed. "Your chauffeur has delivered you safely. Have no fear."

Joyce and Alan stepped out of the car and were walking toward the house when Alan suddenly turned back. "Why don't you drive Lorene home and then come back and pick me up, Ray?" he asked. "It's not far from here."

"Is that for your benefit or mine, pal?" Ray asked.

"Both of ours, of course!" Alan called back.

"Righto! See you in about ten minutes."

"Take your time!" Alan shouted as the car drove off.

"What a character he is, Lorene. You can't appreciate him as I do though. I live with him, and you know what they say—you never really know a man until you've lived with him."

Lorene laughed at the deliberate twist of the meaning and said, "He's a nice guy. Joyce is very much in love with him."

"What about the movies?" Ray asked, changing the subject suddenly.

"What about them?" she asked.

"Do you like them?"

"Yes, very much. Why?"

"Have you seen *Riding High* yet?" he asked. "It just came out about two weeks ago. It has some great stars—Rita Ford, Dennis Hale, and Jack Nickles.

"No, I haven't. Have you?"

"No, and it's supposed to be wonderful. All three of the stars are wonderful actors. I don't want to miss it."

"It's playing in the neighborhood now," Lorene replied.

"Would you like to see it?"

"But I think tomorrow is the last night," she added.

"Well, if two dates in one week aren't too much for you, would you like to go with me?"

"But you have to take such a big trip in from New Jersey," she said. He had told her where he lived. "It's too much to ask you to do," she protested half-heartedly. "And then going back too."

"I'll worry about that. Will you go?"

"Yes, if you'd like."

"I'd like very much. And thank you for being so concerned. Actually, I have a college friend whose parents took a place in

Atlantic Beach for the summer. I can stay with him overnight so I won't have to drive back and forth to Jersey." He took his eyes off the road for a moment to stare at her.

Lorene felt a chill run through her spine.

He brought the car to a halt in front of her house and, after helping her out, walked to the front door with her.

"Will eight o'clock be all right?" he asked.

"That's fine. I think the movie starts at 8:45."

"I'll see you then."

"Good night, Ray, and thank you for a lovely evening," she said softly.

"Good night, Lorene. It's been wonderful for me too."

He stood looking at her for a moment, a deep penetrating glance that made her, once again, shiver. She thought he was going to kiss her, but he simply turned and walked back to the car. Her eyes followed his tall, well-formed physique and admired his broad, manly back and large powerful hands.

He's all man, she thought, almost wishing he hadn't turned and left. *I wish he wasn't so gosh-darned sexy.* She put her key in the door lock and looked back as Ray started his car and drove off. *I wish it were tomorrow night already*, she thought as she opened the door and went in.

Chapter 5

The next morning presented her calling card with fine streams of sunlight filtering through the partially drawn blinds. Lorene turned in her bed, stretched her arms, and with her eye followed the sunbeam to the window and out to the cloudless sky.

What a beautiful day it will be! she thought. *A wonderful Sunday.* She sat up in bed and shook her head. The cobwebs of sleep were difficult to throw as she realized that she might as well get up and wondered what time it was. She reached for the night table and turned the clock toward her.

"Oh, my gosh! It's ten thirty!" she exclaimed.

Quickly she washed and dressed, and in fifteen minutes she bounded down the stairs sounding somewhat like a small herd of elephants as her loafers slapped against each tread.

"Good morning," she called as she raced into the dining room. "Am I very late?" On Sundays, breakfast was in the dining room rather than the kitchen.

Gloria and Bob, just completing their coffee, looked up in unison. Having Lorene late for breakfast the morning after a date was no novelty. In fact, it was customary for her to sleep late without having an excuse to do so.

"Good morning, honey," Gloria said as she placed two slices of bread in the toaster. "Breakfast will be ready in a minute."

"I only want toast and coffee this morning, Mom. I don't feel much like eating."

"Get in late last night?" Bob asked as he emptied his cup.

"Not too bad. About one thirty, I think," she replied.

"How was your date?" he asked.

"Very nice. Ray is a swell fellow. We went to the auto races. They were thrilling. You really should go yourself sometime."

"I've seen them, but I can't say I ever cared for them much." He poured himself a second cup of coffee and commenced to sip it.

"You should go with Ray," she said animatedly. "He knows just about all there is to know about cars, I guess, and he really makes it exciting with his descriptions of what's been done to them. Did you know that the drivers are strapped in and wear helmets and the tops of the cars are completely reinforced, and the spring suspensions are changed and the tires are of different sizes and—"

"Hold on now," Bob interrupted her. "You're beginning to sound like an advertisement. Your old dad may not be hep to everything, but I know a bit too."

"Sorry, Dad. I got carried away."

"About your date too?" Gloria asked innocently, surmising as much from her daughter's attitude.

"Well, I've only seen him once so far, so that's an unfair question." She eyed the sugar bowl and, realizing she couldn't reach it, asked, "Will you pass the sugar, Dad?"

"By that last remark," he began as he handed the sugar bowl to her, "are we to gather that your intentions are to see him again?" Watching his daughter's expression, he knew the answer even before she replied and realized that he was going to have a difficult time ahead of him.

"Why not?" she answered. "Ray's a nice boy and good company. In fact, I'm seeing him tonight."

"Tonight?" Bob was taken aback. This he didn't expect, not so soon.

"Why so surprised?" Lorene asked.

"I just didn't think you'd be seeing him so soon," he lied. "You've never done that with anyone else."

"Ray's different, and there's always a first time," she answered. "We have a date for next Friday too. We're going to the midget races."

"Do you think that's wise?" Bob asked, thinking perhaps the fatherly touch would be more appropriate at a time like this. In any event, it was worth a try.

"What exactly do you mean, Dad?" She was evidently confused.

"I mean, do you think it's wise to spend so much time with this boy?" After all, you're a good-looking girl, and there are plenty of other dates around. Why devote three nights out of seven to this one? That's almost half of the week." He tried to make it sound casual, but he realized it had fallen flat.

"Why?" she began. "Because he's nice, I like him, he likes me, and we enjoy each other's company."

"What about all your other boy friends?" he asked.

"What about them?"

"When will you see them?" He glanced at Gloria, but her expression was quizzical; she obviously didn't understand the reason for the inquisition. It was usual for her to remain quiet during one of these father-daughter discussions, interfering only when she thought it necessary to maintain peace. Every house has its referee, and she was it in her home. She did not choose to assume this role; it was thrust upon her of necessity since her easygoing nature, in contrast with that of her husband, withstood a great deal before losing itself in irrational tantrums. She had continually maintained that there was no need for an argument between two intelligent people—a discussion should suffice—and she was still hoping to prove her theory correct despite the lack of cooperation she received.

"They'll just have to wait until next week. Anyway, I have a date with Ira for this Saturday."

'Well, you've made your dates with this Ray fellow for this week already so nothing can be done, but from now on don't tie yourself down to one boy so much."

"I don't understand you, Dad. What's all the fuss about? I'm not marrying the boy; I'm just dating him." She shrugged her shoulders and again stirred the sugar she had placed in her coffee cup.

"Marry him! I should say not." He slammed his fist on the table. "You've got plenty of time to think of marriage."

"Bob!" Now it was time for Gloria to get involved. Bob's outburst had been to her the symbol of war, and it was up to her to step in and wave the white flag. "What in the world is the matter with you? All Lorene did was make a couple of dates. You're acting as if a calamity has struck."

"It's just that I didn't particularly like the boy," he lied. "I was hoping she wouldn't see him again, but then she calmly announced two more dates and, well …" He turned to Lorene. "I'm sorry," he apologized. "I didn't mean to blow up at you. But I'm not feeling too well this morning, anyway."

"What didn't you like about him?" Lorene asked "Why, you hardly know him. You couldn't have spoken to him more than five minutes. Besides, you've always told me to meet lots of people, go out with a lot, and have a good time going to many different places. Ray is taking me to places I haven't been to before," she said a bit too loudly.

"You needn't raise your voice to me, young lady. Let's drop this conversation right now. I told you I didn't feel well."

"I'm not raising my voice," she said quietly, hoping that she was covering the quiver in her throat. "I only want to know why you're being so unfair for no reason."

Normally Lorene would not be upset if one of her parents didn't like her date, but she felt that Ray was different. She liked him too much.

"I said I didn't want to discuss it anymore," he answered. "I want you to see as little of this boy as possible from now on. Do you understand?" He waited a minute for an answer. "Do you understand?" he shouted as he stood up.

Lorene could control herself no longer. The tears streamed down her face as she turned to meet his staring eyes. She had always been an extremely sensitive child, and a conflict of this kind invariably left her in a tearful state.

"I understand that you want me to obey you blindly because you are my father and you say so!" she cried, "But I'm not a child. If you have a good reason then I'll listen to it, but to be so unjustly prejudiced and expect me to 'obey'—that I don't understand. I don't understand at all, and I won't listen. I refuse to listen because I like Ray, a lot, and he's the first boy I really am looking forward to being with."

"Bob, I think we've had quite enough of this scene," Gloria interjected. But neither Bob nor Lorene paid any attention to her. Both were too emotionally involved.

"You dare to speak to your father in such a tone?" Bob barked. "You have so little respect for me as to disregard my wish? I don't ask much of you. Now I ask for this one thing, and you are fighting me!" Bob was still shouting and becoming more and more angry as he spoke.

"I spoke to you in a tone no worse than the one you used on me," she sobbed. "And, as for respect, I'm not disregarding your wish, only your command."

"Get out of this room!" he ordered, waving his arm in the direction of the door. "Get out and go to your room and don't come down again until you're ready to apologize!"

Lorene turned and fled quickly. Her sobs were audible until she slammed the door to her room.

Gloria turned toward Bob. "I don't even know what to say to you!" she exclaimed. "Your actions were childish. You should be the one to apologize, not your daughter. What got into you, Bob? I've never seen you act this way before."

"Are you going to start too?" he asked as he sank wearily into his chair.

"You're the one who started all this. No one else," she replied.

"I'm only trying to protect her, to see to it that she enjoys herself and doesn't make mistakes. Yet she turns on me and condemns me for it."

"What has she done that she must be protected from?" Gloria queried. "Three dates with a new beau?"

"A boy I don't like," he said.

"Why?"

"I just don't like him."

"That's no reason, and you know it. Even if it were, perhaps she's infatuated with this new boy. So she'll see him a little more often than she should at first and then that will be the end," she reasoned.

"I—I guess you're right. You seem to understand these things better than I do. I guess I overreacted." He cradled his head in his arms, and for a few moments he didn't speak. "Did ... did I make an awful scene?"

"You certainly did. An inexcusable one."

"I'm sorry, truly I am. I got carried away. It's just that I felt so strongly about her seeing this boy. Where are you going?" he asked as Gloria walked out of the room.

"Upstairs to try to patch up this mess." She turned back and asked, "Or would you rather go?"

"No, no, you go. Tell her that I'm sorry. That I lost my temper because … because I wasn't feeling well."

"I'll cover for you," she answered. "But from now on think before you speak. Remember, she's still young and can't see things through your mature eyes. She's a girl, a young woman, and quite emotional. I believe that she thinks she might fall in love with this young man. Trying to dissuade her against him might well have a reverse action at this stage of the game. You wouldn't want that to happen, would you?"

"Oh, my God, no! Not that!" he replied emphatically.

"Why are you so vehement, Bob? What is it you're not telling me?

"Nothing, nothing at all. I just don't like him. You'd better go to her now."

Gloria started up the stairway, which was carpeted in a thick gray broadloom, as was the rest of the house. As a result, her footsteps were barely audible. She knocked on Lorene's closed door and called out to her.

"Lorene, honey, it's Mother. May I come in?"

"The door's not locked," she sobbed.

Gloria's heart ached as she saw her daughter lying across her bed crying needlessly about so unimportant a matter as a date. But she remembered all too clearly when, at about the same age, she had wept for a boy whose name she couldn't even remember today. She sat next to Lorene and gently caressed her hair.

"I'm here, for your father, to say I'm sorry," she said softly.

"Why didn't he come himself?" Lorene asked.

"He's a proud man, Lorene."

"That's a good escape." She sat up and blew her nose gently in a handkerchief.

"It's not an escape," Gloria insisted. "He knew I could say it better than he could."

"Oh, Mom!" She flung her arms around her mother's neck and buried her head in her shoulder.

"Now, now. None of that," Gloria said. "Your father is sorry. He didn't mean most of what he told you. He was upset, not feeling too well this morning, and he truly did not feel you should give so much time to one person. He didn't intend to make such an issue about it, but you persisted in debating his every statement. He loves you, honey, and wants only the best for you. His only fault is that he tries too hard to see that you understand and to protect you."

"But I felt I was one hundred percent right," Lorene protested.

"No one is one hundred percent right at any time. You were both one hundred percent stubborn," she joked.

"Maybe you're right. But honestly, Mom, Ray is really a very nice boy. I don't know what Dad has against him or why, but Ray is tops in my book."

"Well, if you think so, honey, I'll take your word for it."

"You're swell, Mom, the best there is."

"So is your dad, darling. He means well. You'll never find a better father anywhere, or I a better husband."

"I know that. Do you mind my seeing Ray, Mom?

"Not if you want to. If he's not the boy you think he is, you're mature enough to find it out for yourself, soon enough."

"Thanks for having confidence in me," she replied sincerely.

"Now, wash your face and come downstairs," Gloria suggested.

"It will be very awkward."

"Just try to pretend that it didn't happen, Lorene. By tonight it will all be forgotten."

"Okay, I'll be down in a minute."

"You'd better hurry or we won't get in a full day at the beach. It's going to be a scorcher today."

"Be down in a flash."

Gloria closed the door behind her and found Bob in the dining room where she had left him. He looked up as she entered, a questioning expression on his face.

"It's all right now," she reassured him.

"What did you tell her?" He was anxious to know if he was still in the doghouse.

"I merely explained the situation. She's really quite a mature young lady, you know."

"Does she forgive me?"

"Of course. I told her that we'd leave for the beach in a few minutes. You'd better get ready."

"Yes, I'd better. A day at the beach should be very nice. Can I help you prepare lunch?"

"Nope, just get yourself set," she answered.

"All right, honey." He walked over to her and put his hands on her shoulders. "Thanks," he said, "for everything." She tilted her face up to meet his lips. Gloria remembered that he used to kiss her like that when they were engaged, and she liked it so much that she came back for a second try.

Chapter 6

As they crossed over the Atlantic Beach Bridge, the breeze carried the smell of the salt water and sand to them. They had driven in silence for the majority of the ride, but now Bob interrupted it.

"Just get a whiff of the air," he said. "Looks like it will be a wonderful beach day."

"I can't wait to stretch out in the sun," Gloria replied.

They continued on slowly, the heavy traffic deterring their progress.

"Looks like everyone's going to the beach today," Lorene said idly. "The roads are jammed."

"It was just fourteen years ago," Gloria replied as they reached the end of the bridge, "that they expanded the old bridge, so I'm told. And today it looks like it will have to be widened again."

"Engineering can barely manage to keep up with the progress of the times," Bob remarked.

They drove on slowly until they reached the front gates of the Surfside Cabana Club and then wove their way through the parking lanes to the main entrance.

"All out," Bob commanded as the valet approached and handed him a ticket for his car.

Inside the club were sixteen lines of twenty cabanas each, running perpendicular to the ocean. The first and second rows faced each other, as did the third and fourth, and so on to the last, with expanses of approximately fourteen feet of sand between them.

The cabana fronts rotated in order—red, yellow, blue, orange, and green—as they progressed from the first to the last. A wooden walkway three feet in width ran along the entire length of each lane directly in front of the roofed porch area allotted to each cabana. Every cabana was of the same size, with three rooms consisting of two dressing rooms (really, dressing areas, since they were very small), one on either side of and directly behind the main area used for storing chairs, lounges, tables, dishes, a radio, and so forth. Behind each dressing room was another section, one containing a shower and the other a bathroom.

The Ruthers were in row C, the third cabana from the front. All around them were their friends of the last six years who had deliberately maintained their cabanas together for convenience's sake. There wasn't a weekend that passed without a bridge or canasta game or two. There wasn't an hour gone by without laughter from at least a few as a new joke was told. Lorene enjoyed herself with the children of her parents' innumerable acquaintances, but her best times were when she walked along the waterfront to visit her own friends at their various clubs. The cabana clubs stood alongside one another, meeting at their extremities for the few miles covering the entire shore of the beach. From the outside, visitors found that entrance was impossible unless they had membership cards. But in the interior, there were no fences to divide one club from another, making it possible to travel the length of the beach at the water's edge and enter any club desired. Lorene wasn't in the mood to walk this day, so she lay on the lounge looking up at the sun and vainly attempting to doze. Finally, Bob approached her.

"Getting hungry?" he asked as he sat down on the edge of the footrest.

"Sort of," she replied.

"I'll ask Mother to unpack the sandwiches now. Any preference?" he asked.

She sat up, elbowing her way as she did so. "I don't think I feel like a sandwich, Dad. A hot dog with plenty of mustard is more my speed, and those French-fried potatoes smell delicious." The hot dog stand was close enough that the aroma could not be missed.

"What's this I hear about frankfurters and French fries?" Gloria asked as she joined them.

"Lorene isn't in the mood for a sandwich," Bob said. "She has other foodstuffs in mind."

"Well, get it out of your mind," Gloria replied, "and immediately. I made roast beef, salami, ham, and tuna fish sandwiches, and there's no need for them to go to waste."

"Oh, now Gloria," Bob said. "Lorene can have the frankfurter if she wants."

Gloria was obviously annoyed. "Bob!" she replied angrily.

"There are plenty of times when I get a yearning for a particular thing," he explained. "Here, Lorene," he reached into the pocket of his bathing trunks and removed some change, "go get what you want."

Gloria watched Lorene disappear in the direction of the snack bar, and when she was out of sight Gloria turned to Bob. "What are you trying to do? Make up for how badly you acted earlier? If so, that's not the way to do it. You are spoiling her. And you have complete disregard for me. I prepared a lunch for all of us."

"Can't help it. I love her," he answered. "Besides, you are right—I want to make up for this morning. I want to show her I'm not the bad guy."

"You're always doing everything for Lorene," Gloria commented.

"What she asked wasn't so unreasonable," he replied. "You're annoyed because you made all the sandwiches. We can finish them for lunch tomorrow. It's not so terrible."

"That isn't the point, Bob," she insisted.

"What difference does it make?" he asked. "Come on now, let's forget the whole thing and dig into that food. I'm hungry."

When Lorene returned two hours later, Bob asked, "Where have you been, pet?"

"I had lunch," she explained, "and then stayed around to watch the afternoon dance lessons. They were doing the cha-cha."

"Would you like to take lessons?" he asked her.

"I don't think so. I know how to do most of the dances."

"Well, if you change your mind, let me know," he said.

"Why don't you and Mom take them, Dad?" she asked. "Mom loves to dance."

"I can't stand it," he answered. "I have two left feet and no sense of rhythm at all."

"Have you gone in the water yet?" Lorene asked, changing the subject.

"Yes, but I'm ready for another dip if you are," he replied.

"Be with you in half a sec," she called as she raced into the cabana for her bathing cap.

Within a few minutes, the two of them had splashed into the ocean. The breakers were low, affording an excellent opportunity to swim. Normally the waves off the Atlantic Beach shore were quite high, forcing the bathers to merely dive under, jump over, or ride in on the breaker. Bob and Lorene swam and splashed each other for a while, carrying on like children, and then headed back to the cabana.

"Just look at that suit!" Lorene exclaimed, pointing at a woman a few yards to their right. "Isn't it beautiful?" It was a black, strapless, wool number, form fitted throughout, with a gold strap extending from the left-hand side of the back over the right shoulder.

"It sure is, but a better figure would improve upon it," he commented.

"I saw that suit in a window in one of the Cedarhurst shops," Lorene replied.

"It would look wonderful on *you*, hon."

"It's awfully expensive, Dad."

"Do you really like it?" he asked.

"And how!"

"Remind me tonight to give you the money so that you can go get it Monday. You still have half the season to wear it," he rationalized.

"Thanks a million, Dad!" She threw her arms around him and gave him a big kiss.

"That's enough thanks for me," he said sincerely, thinking how well he knew how to make his daughter happy.

"You can be so wonderful," she replied and then added, "sometimes."

"Always remember," he said, "whatever I do, I do because I think it's best for you. Your welfare is my only motivation."

"I'll try to remember, Dad. But, please, try to listen to what I have to say. There are two sides to a story, you know."

"I will. But come on," he answered. "Your mother is waiting. I think she finished her canasta game."

Chapter 7

Helen quietly closed the side door behind her and walked toward the kitchen. She was a large, six-foot tall, broad-shouldered African American woman whose appearance was more masculine than feminine. Her breadth equaled that of a two-hundred-pound male, and her waist, if not marked by a bright red belt, would have been indistinguishable. Her clothes were always ill fitting, too tight or too short, and her bronzed skin played peek-a-boo within the varied open seams on the sides of her dresses. She was a gem, though—a wonderful, honest, reliable cleaning woman who had been letting herself into the Ruthers' house five mornings a week for the past three years. The family had become quite attached to her and she to them.

This Friday morning, in addition to her usual attire, she boasted a pair of sunglasses that she persisted in wearing despite being indoors. Gloria was in the kitchen stacking the breakfast dishes when she heard Helen enter.

"Good morning," she said, turning from the sink to see her.

"Good mornin', Mrs. Ruthers," Helen answered moving, quickly in the direction of the maid's room off to one side of the kitchen.

"Just a minute!" Gloria commanded kindly. "Will you turn around again?"

Helen obeyed slowly, raising her hand to her eyes as she did so.

"Why the sunglasses?" Gloria asked.

"I—I bumped myself on a kitchen cabinet door. I has a black eye, Mrs. Ruthers."

"Did he hit you again?" Gloria guessed. For five years Helen had been going with a man much older than herself who needed little excuse to relieve himself of the tension of his drunken stupors.

"Yes," she answered quietly, "last night."

Gloria was sympathetic. "What happened this time?"

"We have an argument, Mrs. Ruthers. He got sore and let me have it."

"Why do you take it from him, Helen? Why do you let your boyfriend do this to you all the time?" she questioned.

"I'm not goin' let him anymore. I'm leavin' him."

"Good for you, Helen. It's about time. I honestly don't know how you stood it up to now. You're a nice girl. You don't need him. Now come here," she requested kindly, "and let me see that eye."

Helen walked over and removed her glasses. The eye was very bad, swollen and black from the top of her eyebrow to the tip of her nose.

"That's terrible!" Gloria said, horrified. "You make sure you take care of this today. Keep putting cold compresses on it."

"I will, Mrs. Ruthers. Thank you."

"That no-good drunken boyfriend of yours ought to be ashamed of himself," Gloria added. "I wish you could hit him back."

"I did last night, Mrs. Ruthers. If you think my eye is bad, you oughta see his."

Gloria started to laugh but, realizing it would be in bad taste, bit the inside of her bottom lip to keep the smile controlled. She turned back to the dishes and simply said, "He deserved it."

"Please, Mrs. Ruthers," Helen pleaded, "don't say nothin' to Miss Lorene. I wouldn't want her to know."

"But she'll see you," Gloria protested.

"I'll wear my glasses all day. I kin tell her my eyes hurt me."

"All right, Helen, if that's what you want."

"Thank you, Mrs. Ruthers."

She turned toward the maid's room and walked in quickly. Gloria knew she was putting on her freshly starched uniform, preparing to do her day's work. Gloria truly pitied her; she knew what a nice girl she really was.

When Helen emerged from the room, looking much better in a well-fitting dress, Gloria had an idea.

"Helen," she said, "if you have no place to go, you can live here for a while. We have the extra room and bath."

"That's very nice of you, Mrs. Ruthers, but I'm gonna rent a room. I know where I kin get me one."

"That's up to you," Gloria answered, "but the offer is open whenever you should want to accept."

"I'll remember it," Helen replied as she set about collecting her dustcloth, mop and vacuum cleaner. "But I don't think I'll be comin' here. I has other plans."

Gloria dropped the subject then and set about completing her chores around the house. Then, donning her sun hat and work gloves, she went out to the garden to do some weeding. When the prospect of caring for a garden had first greeted her, she was appalled at the idea. "Not me," she had said. "I hate that sort of work. If you want land, Bob, you'll have to get a gardener to care for it or do the odd jobs yourself." But that was six years ago, and in time Gloria had come to realize that working in the garden was very relaxing. She loved sitting on the cool lawn clad in Bermuda shorts and a cotton shirt, kicking off her shoes and digging her toes into the green grass. In this position, weeding or pulling crabgrass was more enjoyment than work.

She had been working diligently for about half an hour when she paused to relax, and lighting a cigarette, she dug her elbows into the ground and threw her weight backward, taking a deep, lung-filling breath as she did so. She remained that way, sprawled out as if getting a suntan, until her cigarette was finished.

"Good morning, Mrs. Ruthers."

She turned her head to see the intruder.

"Oh, Joe!" she exclaimed as she scrambled to her feet. She had been so absorbed that she had forgotten that she was working on the front lawn. She felt that she must have appeared rather unladylike lying on the lawn that way.

"You looked so comfortable I hated to disturb you," he said.

He was a gaunt man in his late twenties who oftentimes appeared too weak to push the mail sack before him. His hair was almost pure blond and inevitably tussled, giving him a carefree appearance. His eyes, however, small and blue and deeply set, were penetrating and displayed wisdom and understanding far beyond his years. He was a quiet man, talkative only when constantly prodded.

"That's all right," she explained. "I should be getting back to my gardening anyway. Any mail for me today?"

"Just one letter," he replied as he handed it to her. "Well," he added "I'm a little late so I'd better be moving on."

"Joe?"

"Yes, Mrs. Ruthers?"

"Do you mind if I ask you a sort of personal question?"

"That all depends."

"Is there any truth to the rumor that you may be … " She didn't quite know how to say it. "That you may be fired?"

"It's true, all right." His eyes dropped, and he stared at his feet while he nervously shifted his weight from one leg to the other.

"Why?" she asked.

"It's a long story, Mrs. Ruthers. You see," he began, "when you apply for a civil service job they give you a very complete questionnaire to fill out. They have just about every question you can imagine on it. One of them asks if you were ever arrested. Naturally, I said no. I completely forgot that when I was eighteen years old, I was with a friend of mine who had a BB gun. We were on the roof of an apartment house in New York City. My friend shot the gun, and then I shot it. I thought I was shooting it into the air, but a BB hit a lady. She wasn't hurt badly, but we were both taken to the police station. She pressed charges. The judge released us with a warning and a good lecture. And we had to pay her doctor fees. I had forgotten it because there was no trial. But when Civil Service investigated it, they found this record and now they say I lied in order to get the job."

"What will they do?" She was surprised with the story and thought it was a rather trivial reason for a man to be discharged, especially since the deception was committed in innocence and was a minor infraction.

"They're reviewing the case now, but it looks as if I'll be fired."

"How terrible. I'm sorry, Joe," she said sympathetically.

"Thank you, Mrs. Ruthers."

"What will you do?" she asked.

"I don't know yet." He was staring at his feet again.

"Would a petition help you at all?"

"No, I don't think so, but thanks for being so concerned." He moved on slowly, pretending to sort the mail in his hand as he walked, but Gloria realized it was only a pretense at preoccupation.

She returned to her weeding, thinking of the injustice of the situation and hoping that he wouldn't be fired after all. *Men go unpunished for far worse things*, she thought. *Poor Joe. I hope things work out for him.*

Chapter 8

It was two o'clock in the morning and as clear and bright as it would be at eight. The sky was blanketed with a quilt of stars, and the full moon rested, like a pillow, toward one corner.

"What a beautiful night," Lorene sighed as the car stopped before her house, "and what a wonderful evening I've had. Those midget races were better than I expected, but they still weren't as good as the stocks were last week."

"Have you really enjoyed yourself?" Ray asked.

"Very much," she replied with a deep sigh, breathing in the warm evening air. "How about you?"

"I never knew there was a girl like you," he answered seriously. "And because of you, I've had one of the best evenings I remember in a long time."

"You're being very gallant tonight, sir, and very complimentary, but I'm mighty skeptical about believing such flattery after so short a time."

"That's not very nice to say." He was a bit hurt. "Don't you believe me?"

"Yes and no. I've met too many boys with a wonderful line to believe it all." Though she was skeptical of his sincerity, inwardly she longed to believe that he really did feel the way he said he did.

"This is no line, Lorene. I've never lied to a girl in my life," he replied. "That's one clean mark on my slate. I never told a girl I cared for her if I didn't or that I enjoyed myself if it wasn't true."

"I want to believe you, Ray. You're very nice, and I like you and being with you." She opened her purse and drew out a cigarette.

"I've got a light," he said quickly. He pulled out a blue butane lighter and pressed on the lever. A flame appeared. In the glow of the flame, he scanned her face carefully. "You're quite beautiful, you know. Beautiful and intelligent and pure. That's my Lorene." Then he lit her cigarette.

She didn't know what to say.

"Maybe I can prove that I mean it," he added. "Do you see this?" He reached into his pocket and withdrew a large, dull coin. He handed it to her.

"It's a silver dollar," she said as she examined it in her palm.

"Not just a silver dollar. It's my lucky piece. Originally it was my father's. He carried it with him throughout the Second World War. He was a gunner, you know. Do you see the scratches around the outer rim?"

She nodded as she noted the various marks and ran her thumbnail over them.

"Each of these stands for a mission that my dad was on. He went through quite a bit, but that coin was with him throughout. I want you to have it now, Lorene."

"Me? But why?" She was surprised.

"Because I want you to have it," he repeated, "as a token of my … because I like you."

"But I can't take this, Ray," she protested. "It was your dad's, and it's your lucky piece. And we have known each other for such a short time. We've only had a few dates. I don't want to take anything from you."

"It has been a short time, but I feel like I've known you a lot longer. And I know how I feel about you. I want you to have it. Please take it, Lorene. I don't need any more luck now that I've met you."

"Do you really mean that?"

"I was never good with words, and now I'm finding it even harder to express myself. I know that this is only the third time we've seen each other, but I feel something for you that I have never felt for anyone else. I hope that this something, whatever it is, is mutual and that I'm not just another date to you."

"You're not," she assured him. "And that something is certainly mutual."

"Then you'll keep the silver dollar?" He was relieved.

"If you really want me to."

"I do. Really, I do."

"But on one condition," she added.

"What's that?" He was puzzled.

"If the day should come when you want it back, you have to promise to tell me."

"I promise. But I won't want it back, ever." He pressed his hand against her fingers, closing them tightly about the coin. "Unfortunately," he continued, "because we haven't known each other long enough, that lucky piece can't mean what I'd like it to. So, in the meantime, let's just say it means I more than like you, very much."

"Fair enough," she replied. "But I wish I had something to offer you in return."

"I have a suggestion to make," he said.

"What?"

"How about me picking you up on Monday morning, early? We'll go fishing, then swimming, and we'll make a day of it."

"That sounds wonderful." She was enthusiastic. "Except …"

"Except what?"

"Dad. He'll be all upset. He thought I was seeing too much of you as it was this week."

"Doesn't he like me?" Ray questioned, a bit hurt. "Did I do something to offend him?"

"Oh, that isn't it," she assured him. "It's just that he feels I shouldn't confine myself to one boy so much."

"Funny, my mother said almost the same thing. She thinks I should be seeing lots of girls. But the important thing is, do *you* want to see *me*? Because I want to see *you*."

"Yes, I do," she replied and then added, "very much."

"Then that settles it because I want to see you, every day if that's possible. I only have one month until school starts, so let's make the most of it."

"That's fine with me," she answered. "I'm not really worried about Dad anyway. He's all bark and no bite."

"I'm sure he's very nice," Ray said.

"He is, in his own stubborn way."

"Don't forget about our dates for next Friday and Saturday nights," he reminded her. "Let's make it for dinner first on Saturday, okay?" he asked.

"Fine, and don't worry, I won't forget. What time will you pick me up on Monday morning?"

"Early, about eight. That all right?"

"Fine. I'm looking forward to it. I've never been fishing. But I'd better be getting in now, Ray. It's very late."

"I hate to say good night, but I don't want your folks angry with me for keeping you out all night. Mustn't start with two strikes against me, you know." He smiled, and she laughed lightly. Then, turning her face toward his, their glances remained fixed for an instant.

"Good night, Ray, and thank you for a wonderful evening," she said.

"Good night, Lorene." He bent his head down toward her, and their lips met gently in a tender caress. Then, suddenly, he pulled her close and buried his lips deeply into hers. They embraced with all the furor of those in love. His right hand tenderly moved slowly through her short brown hair and then gently caressed her forehead. The fingers of his left hand moved slowly over her soft neck and shoulders. They both recognized the fury of their passion, but neither spoke of or admitted it.

"I'd better go in now," Lorene said finally, "before Dad comes out looking for me."

"Okay," he answered softly. "Just one more for the road." He placed his hand under her chin, tilted her face up to meet his, and kissed her gently, tenderly. The violence of the prior embrace was gone.

"Come on," he said. "I'll take you to the door."

They walked slowly, hand in hand, while in her free fist she clutched the silver dollar and thought how lucky it would be for her too.

I have to be the luckiest girl in the world, she thought. *How could life be any better?*

CHAPTER

Chapter 9

It was Monday morning. Lorene, unaccustomed as she was to rising early, especially during the summer months when her only preoccupation was keeping herself from becoming bored, was quite energetic as she bounded down the stairs and raced into the kitchen. Earlier in the season she had taken a clerical position with a lens company on Fifth Avenue in New York City, but she had become despondent with the heat in a matter of weeks and so had retired quickly into a state of laxity, which in due course transformed itself into idleness. Gloria was upset that Lorene would be lounging around, but Bob supported her and agreed that she had worked hard enough at school all year and deserved a break.

"I've only got time for a cup of coffee this morning, Mom," she gushed as she pulled her chair up to the table.

"And to what do we owe the unexpected pleasure of your company at seven thirty in the morning?" Bob asked jokingly.

"I've got a date." She gulped down the last of her orange juice.

"If you don't slow down," Gloria warned," the only date you'll have will be with the doctor for a case of indigestion."

"What sort of date do you have at seven thirty a.m.?" Bob questioned.

"I'm going fishing."

"Fishing? With whom? You've never gone fishing before."

"I forgot to tell you, Dad," she lied. She had deliberately neglected telling him in hopes of avoiding a scene. "Ray's taking me. He'll be here any minute." She dropped a spoonful of sugar into her coffee and stirred it rapidly.

"Forgot to tell me? You mean you forgot on purpose." He was angry.

"Now, Dad, why would I do that?"

"You know how I feel, Lorene."

"Summer vacation's half over, Dad. Let a girl have some fun." She fumbled in her pocketbook. "Besides, I've never been fishing."

"I never knew that you even cared to go before this young scalawag asked you."

"Now, Bob," Gloria cautioned, "let's not repeat our scene of last week."

"But such complete disregard for my wishes, Gloria!" he argued. "She knows I asked her to see him as little as possible, and now she's going out with him again." He turned toward Lorene. "How many more dates have you made with him for this week?"

"Not many."

"Don't be evasive, Lorene. I asked you, how many?"

"Just two more, for Friday and Saturday nights." She continued to fumble in her purse. "Now, what did I do with my cigarettes?"

"Two more? That's three again this week. I won't stand for it, Lorene."

"Dad!" she exclaimed, exasperated.

"Lorene, your father is right," Gloria interjected. "Aside from the fact that your father dislikes Ray, you have no business seeing one boy so often. You're too young to tie yourself down so much."

"Do you dislike him too, Mom?" she asked despairingly.

"Well, I really don't know him well enough," she replied

truthfully. "I've spoken with him briefly when he came to pick you up. He seemed nice enough."

"Then how does Dad know him well enough? He only spoke with him briefly too," she protested.

"Your father is a very good judge of character. He always has been. He sat and talked with Ray for a few minutes and developed an opinion. But, as I said, aside from that—"

"I know," Lorene interrupted. "I really shouldn't tie myself down to one boy. But did you ever stop to think that maybe now I'd *like* to be tied down? I'm past eighteen. I've finished a year in college, and I know what I want."

"And just what do you think you want?" Gloria asked.

"Maybe Ray. I'm not sure yet."

"You're not serious, Lorene. You can't be!" Bob said. "Why in the world should you pick that boy?"

"Why did Mother pick you?"

"That was different. Your mother and I fell in love, and my intentions were serious. I wanted your mother to marry me."

"Maybe Ray's intentions are the same."

"Has he said so?" Gloria asked.

"Not exactly, but look." She removed the silver dollar and placed it on the table. She had hesitated to show it to them earlier since she was fearful of her father's reaction. But this seemed to be the right time. "That was his father's during the war; each scratch on the rim signifies another mission. This was Ray's good-luck piece, but he gave it to me."

"Oh, fiddlesticks," Bob said, skeptical. "I didn't think you were so naïve. The boy undoubtedly has twenty-five of these and gives every girl the same line. I know boys. He's after one thing, and he's just working his way up to it."

"It's no line, Dad. It's true," Lorene argued.

"So what? In one month, off he'll go to Troy, hundreds of miles away. You'll never see or hear from him again. And where will you be left? By yourself, that's where, without even a date because you stopped seeing them all for this summertime Romeo."

"You're wrong, Dad. It won't be like that at all." She quickly picked up the coin and placed it back in her purse.

"Lorene, honey. Your father and I don't want to see you get hurt. Even if this boy is the right one for you, he still has another year of school before graduation. If you think this is the right thing, give yourself time to prove it, and the only way to prove it is to continue dating others so that you have a good basis for comparison," Gloria reasoned.

"I won't stop seeing everyone else, Mom, but I just don't enjoy myself with anyone else since I've met Ray."

"Have it your own way, Lorene," Bob said, "but remember when the fall comes that we've warned you. This boy hasn't told you that he loves you, hasn't proposed marriage, yet you're ready to give up every other date."

"I didn't say that, Dad. You're twisting my words."

"Don't count your chickens before they're hatched, honey," Gloria said kindly. Her only thought was to keep her daughter from being hurt.

"I won't." She rose and started for the door. "I've got to get going now. I'm sorry, Dad, truly I am, but you're being unfair. Ray's very, very nice, and you'd really like him if you'd give him half a chance." She walked out and up the stairs back to her room.

For a few moments, the kitchen was silent. Bob broke the quiet with a low, almost inaudible exclamation.

"I'll never like that boy. He's not for Lorene and never will be."

"Why, Bob?" Gloria asked. "What is it about him that you hate so?" She was obviously confused. This was not like Bob to be so emphatic.

"You'd never understand, Gloria."

"Try me."

"No, not now."

"Then how can I help you if I don't even understand you?"

"Help me?" He was puzzled.

"To break up this romance. That's what you want, isn't it?"

"With all my heart, Gloria, more than anything else in this world."

"I don't understand you, Bob. You've never been so unreasonable before. Perhaps if you got to know Ray better."

"No, no, I won't do that. It won't make a difference."

"Then what is it? Tell me. For God's sake, tell me!" She hadn't raised her voice throughout the previous conversation, but now irritation swept through her as she strove to accept the views of her husband whose attitude she couldn't understand. She had heard about husbands who refused to confide in their wives, but until now their relationship had been of the most intimate nature. They always shared everything. "If you don't tell me, Bob, then there's nothing more I can do. I can't continue to stand by your side when I know with all my heart that Lorene is doing nothing wrong. I can't stand by you unless you explain why you feel so strongly."

"Doing nothing wrong, you say? Isn't seeing this boy so much wrong? Isn't wanting to marry him wrong? Isn't going against her father's wishes wrong?"

"No," she answered simply and quietly.

"*No*? What do you mean *no*? Sometimes I just don't understand you, Gloria. This is your daughter, our daughter, we're discussing, not a stranger."

"She's not wrong in seeing this boy so much, only foolish perhaps. But the young must make their own mistakes. We did. We wouldn't listen to others, and we made our mistakes. Wanting to marry him isn't wrong if he's as nice as she says and she loves him. That, too, may be foolish, but it's not wrong. I remember boys I wanted to marry. How wrong I would have been if I had, but I didn't. I was mature enough to make my decision correctly. So is your daughter. And as for going against her father's wishes, remember that she is hurt, her pride is wounded, and her sense of maturity has been attacked. You're asking her to do something with very little justification or explanation on your part just like you would insist a three-year-old fulfill your command with blind obedience. She's rebelling, and I can't say I blame her."

"I can see what you think of me now," he said angrily. "It's all too clear. You haven't even enough faith in me to be assured I'm acting for the best. After all our years of marriage, our trust in each other, why must you refuse to trust me now?"

"Unless you let me in on your secret grievance, all that I or anyone in my position can see is that you're an unfair, prejudiced man with no basis for your feelings."

"I have a good reason, an excellent one, for not wanting those two to get married, get serious, or even see each other."

"You're talking in circles, Bob, repeating the same thing over and over."

"I can't offer you any further explanation now," he pleaded, "but please, please, have faith in me and help me. Believe me, this union would be a disaster."

"I won't press you any further. But I also can't and won't offer you any support. It would be unfair of you to ask it. When you are ready to tell me the truth, I'll listen and decide what I think is best. Until then, I'll be my own judge and weigh the facts as I see them."

"Please, please," Bob begged, "believe in me."

"Not until you can trust in me. I'm your wife, Bob. You owe me at least that."

"I can't tell you, not yet. Maybe this whole thing will blow over and there will be no need for explanations. All I can say now is that I don't like the boy." He wanted to tell Gloria the truth. More than anything in the world he wanted to tell her. But he was afraid of her reaction, of what she would do, of how she would look at him, and so he was determined to reveal his secret only in desperation and in utter necessity.

"And all I can say is that you're acting like a jealous father unwilling to see his only child taken away from him in marriage."

"That's not it. God help me, I wish it were."

"I'm completely baffled, Bob, completely. What else can it be? You don't even know the boy."

He rose, looked at Gloria for a moment, and then turned to walk slowly toward the front door.

"I know him," he muttered under his breath, too low for Gloria to hear. "I know him only too well. God help me. I brought this upon myself." Aloud he said to Gloria, "I have a train to catch. I've missed the 7:45, so I'll have to get the next one. Are you ready to drive me to the station?" With that he opened the front door and went outside.

When Gloria heard the door close, she sighed and took a handkerchief from her pocket to wipe a tear from her eye. This wasn't like Bob, not at all. Suddenly he was a stranger to her and treating her in the same way.

Chapter 10

The next day was a specimen of summer perfection. The temperature hovered about the ninety-two-degree mark while the humidity remained constant around 40 percent. An ocean breeze had blown in about eleven o'clock in the morning and stirred the trees in sufficient amount to fan the burning rays of the sun and relieve the intensity of the heat. Lorene wore a strapless pink cotton dress with shirring from the waist up and a full-circle petticoat skirt when she appeared for brunch. About her throat was a pink, three-strand pearl choker, and small pearl earrings to match edged her dainty ears. She had just prepared a cream cheese and jelly sandwich and a cup of coffee when Gloria appeared.

"Good morning, lazy bones," she said. "How was the date yesterday?"

"Fine," she answered, biting into the sandwich.

"Want to go to the beach with me today?"

"Not today, Mom. I'm going over to Joyce's house."

"If you don't go, I don't think I will," Gloria answered. "I have a few things to catch up on in the house anyway."

"If you're not going to use the car, do you mind if I take it?"

Gloria thought for a moment and then said, "I suppose it's all right. I don't need it, but be sure to be back in time to pick your dad up at the station."

"Oh, I'll be back way before that." She took her dirty dish and cup, rinsed them out, and put them on the counter. "I'll get started now."

She gave Gloria a fleeting kiss goodbye and whisked out the door in the direction of the garage. Once in the pale-blue-and-white, four-door, hardtop Cadillac, she backed carefully out into the street and headed for Broadway, which she drove along until she came to Sealy Drive. At the bend in the street was Joyce's house. She lived in the town of Lawrence, a more upscale area than Ivy Lane in Woodmere. Lorene pulled into the driveway and parked halfway up its sixty-foot length.

Joyce was waiting in the doorway for her. "I saw you drive up," she explained, and then she added, "Come on up to my bedroom. My mom's having a canasta game this afternoon, and she's busy getting lunch ready for 'the girls,'" she said as she imitated her mother's nasal tones. The girls thought it was funny that their mothers referred to their friends as *the girls* because, in their eyes, these women were far from being girls.

The two girls tromped up the stairs and into Joyce's room. Lorene sat on the desk chair while Joyce perched herself on the edge of the bed. She was an attractive brunette with short cropped hair. Her face was sweet and almost childlike in its roundness. Her body was chubby but far from obese and still well-proportioned in its roundness.

"Well," she asked impatiently, "how have your dates been going? Alan and I have been as curious as wet hens since we found out how often you've been seeing one another."

"He's awfully nice," Lorene replied. "The nicest fellow I've ever met."

"Tell me more," Joyce prodded.

>60

60

"He gave me this the other day." She took out the silver dollar, and as Joyce examined it as though it was the world's rarest diamond, Lorene repeated the story of its origin and significance.

"That's wonderful," Joyce said as she handed it back. "Why, in all the years we've known Ray, he has never given a girl anything. She was lucky if he took her out a second time. Most of his dates were one night only."

"It's wonderful, and then again it's not," Lorene replied thoughtfully.

"What do you mean?" She reached for the pack of cigarettes on her night table. "Have one," she offered.

Lorene shook her head no and waited while Joyce lit her cigarette and found a wrought-iron ashtray on the desk. She placed it on her lap.

"It's my dad, Joyce. I don't know what to do. He's so set against Ray."

"Why?"

"Oh, he gives me a million reasons—he's still in school, too young, no future, et cetera, et cetera, et cetera."

"Don't worry about it," Joyce said. "They're all the same. You should have seen my dad when I told him Alan and I wanted to get engaged. He blew his top. But he settled down when he realized it was inevitable. I think our fathers are just shocked at realizing we're not babies anymore. It's a blow to their egos. They've considered themselves so young all these years."

"But my mother doesn't seem to feel the same," Lorene protested.

"I think mothers remember how they felt when they were our age."

"Maybe you're right," Lorene admitted, "at least I certainly hope you are. Dad's in a terrible way now."

"It will blow over just as soon as he sees and is sure that this is really it."

"Maybe you're right, although I really shouldn't worry at this point," she added thoughtfully.

"What do you mean?"

"Ray hasn't even asked me to get engaged. And he certainly hasn't asked me to marry him. And he may not."

"Want to take a bet on that?" Joyce questioned.

"Definitely not. Why should I defeat my own purposes?"

"Oh, honey, I'm so happy for you," Joyce said. "I am so sure he's going to ask you. We'll be married around the same time, after the boys graduate. I'm sure he'll ask you. I'm positive he'll ask you," she repeated.

"Uh-huh, it will be wonderful if it works out that way. But I don't know what makes you so certain."

"I *am* certain. Just knowing Ray makes me certain. He's never been like this with anyone else. Oh, Lorene, won't it be wonderful? Us being such good friends and the boys liking each other so much? We can be lifelong friends."

"It will be wonderful, just heaven." Lorene sighed thinking not of the friendship with Joyce but of the marriage itself.

Joyce suggested, "Maybe he'll ask you soon so that you can get engaged right away. We could keep each other company during the winter when school is in session."

"I really don't care when he asks me," Lorene replied, "just as long as he does."

With a touch of sympathy in her voice, Joyce asked, "You really have it bad, don't you, kid?"

Lorene nodded.

"What kind of ring do you prefer? A round or square stone? Baguette or marquis?"

And so the girl talk transformed itself to womanly conversation as dreams of the future were aired. Color schemes, furniture, dishes, and home were the prime topics as the problems of the present were disregarded in the interests of the pleasure of what was to come. The hours passed quickly amid such daydreams, but the reality of time caught up to them.

"I can't believe how late it is!" Lorene commented. "I'll have to be going."

"Let's go live on some desert island and get away from it all," Joyce suggested.

Lorene laughed aloud. "You can't get away from it all. You can't get away from things by ignoring them."

"I guess not, but it would be nice to try. Wouldn't it be nice to be somewhere where there are no problems?"

"That brings me right back to my dad, right where we started from today," Lorene noted.

"An excellent time to call the *finis* to the afternoon, then," Joyce replied. "Call me soon."

"I will. So long, Joyce. At least you've given me some hope."

"That's all you need," she called out the door as Lorene headed for the car, "hope and faith."

Chapter 11

Four weeks had passed since the black-eye incident with Helen, and during the interim she had seemed quite happy.

"It's wonderful, Mrs. Ruthers," she had said. "It's the best time I ever had."

"Living all alone?" Gloria had asked, surprised. "Isn't it lonesome for you?"

"I've met lots of people. One fella, a painter, is my boyfriend now. I like him a lot."

"I see," Gloria answered, thinking how childishly this grown woman in her twenties was acting. "I'm glad everything's working out so well for you."

To herself, she had admitted doubt. She hoped that Helen was not meeting the wrong kind of people because she was such a nice person and she hated to see her get mixed up with a bad crowd.

This morning, Helen's usual carefree disposition had disappeared. She seemed lifeless and glum, and in place of the popular melodies that usually flowed from her mouth, her large, thick lips were set in a straight, grim line. Her work for the first three hours had been poor and painstakingly slow. Three or four times she had left what she was doing to spend a few minutes in the bathroom. Finally, Gloria could bear it no longer.

"What is it, Helen?" she asked kindly. "What's the matter with you today? Aren't you feeling well?"

Helen turned quickly and gazed steadily at Gloria's feet. Normally she was extremely loquacious and eager to talk about herself and her problems; now, however, she said simply, "Nothin', ma'am. I'm okay."

"You're certainly not acting it today," Gloria replied. "Are you sure you're feeling all right?" she repeated.

Helen kept gazing at the floor. It was evident that she had something to hide. "I'm not feelin' my best, if that's what you mean," she said slowly.

Standing there, head downcast and completely dejected, she reminded Gloria of a child caught in a bad act. Never before had Helen displayed even the slightest signs of anything other than complete honesty, and now here she was refusing to admit she was sick.

"Why didn't you tell me you weren't well today?" Gloria asked. "You know I'd have excused you. Perhaps you should be home in bed."

"No, Mrs. Ruthers, I don't has to go to bed."

"Well, what is it then? Of course you don't have to tell me, but I was under the impression that our relationship was more than just an employer-employee situation," she said kindly. "You've been working here a number of years. I like you, Helen, and if I can help you in any way—"

"If I tell you, Mrs. Ruthers," Helen started to say, interrupting Gloria. "If I tell you, will you promise to keep it a secret?"

"Who would I tell it to?" Gloria asked.

"I don't know." She raised her head and looked straight at Gloria, revealing very moist eyes glistening under her thick, black eyebrows. "I think I'm goin' to have a baby."

"A baby!" Gloria couldn't believe it. "You're pregnant?" she asked in surprise.

"The doctor isn't sure. I went to see him last night, and he said it was too soon to tell. I'm only two weeks late on my period. But he thinks I am, and I've been so sick, throwin' up all the time. That's why I hasn't been feelin' well."

"Has the doctor given you anything to take? Gloria asked.

"He gave me some pills for throwin' up."

"Are you taking them?"

"Yes, but it hasn't helped much yet."

"What will you do," Gloria asked, "if you are pregnant?"

Helen looked shocked and answered curtly, "I'm not believin' in usin' the knitting needle, if that's what you mean."

"Oh, no, Helen! I wasn't referring to that at all."

Gloria had heard of the extraordinary use of the knitting needle in times like these, though she had never suspected anyone she knew of using such tactics when they had miscarried. Her friends had, however, actually come in contact with the situation many times, and so they had told her the secondhand details, which they had gotten from their domestic help. The knitting-needle abortion was performed by either the girl herself or her boyfriend. Surprisingly enough, the procedure proved most satisfactory, and rarely did a girl become ill from this unsanitary practice.

"I merely meant," Gloria continued, trying to appease the hurt feeling she had created, "what are your plans if you are pregnant?"

"I don't know. I haven't thought about it yet 'cause I'm still not sure."

"Well, look at this realistically," Gloria said. "What other earthly reason could there be for you to be two weeks late? Are you irregular?"

"No."

"And I assume that it is possible"—she emphasized *possible*, not being certain exactly what other word to use—"for you to be pregnant."

"Yes, ma'am, with one of my boyfriends. I'm not tellin' them 'cause I'm not seein' them no more and I don't know which one it was."

"Who will take care of the baby, Helen?"

"I don't know. And like I said, I don't even know who the father is."

"I didn't mean financially; I meant physically."

"I don't know. I can't take care of a baby. I needs to go to work. My mother has passed. Maybe I'll give the baby for adoption. The baby kin have a better life than mine."

"I'm sure everything will work out for you, Helen. You're being very sensible." Then she added, "If there is anything I can do for you, just let me know."

"I will, Mrs. Ruthers. Thank you."

"Now, you take it easy. Don't work too hard until you feel better," Gloria cautioned.

"I won't work too hard. I lost one baby when I was eighteen. Do you think I might lose this one too?"

"Just be careful that you don't injure yourself. You'll be fine."

"I'll be okay, Mrs. Ruthers. Don't you worry."

Gloria left the room. While walking to the kitchen to prepare lunch, she thought of the feeling she had had that Helen was getting in with a bad crowd. *I hoped she'd not be like most of the others in that group*, she thought. *What a pity. She is such a nice girl.*

"Mother?"

"Oh, Lorene, you startled me. I didn't know you were in the kitchen. I was thinking about something, and I must have been completely absorbed."

"I know. I heard," Lorene answered.

"Heard? Heard what?"

"Everything that Helen told you."

"Oh. She didn't want anyone to know," Gloria said.

"I couldn't help it. I was in the next room."

"I'm sorry that you heard," Gloria replied. "Don't let on to Helen that you did."

"I won't. Can I ask you a question, Mother?"

"Sure, what is it?"

"I thought that after her boyfriend gave her the black eye a month ago, she left him. Wasn't that right?"

"That's right."

`"Did she go back to him? Why in the world did she do that when he was so mean to her?" Lorene asked.

"She didn't go back to him," Gloria answered, marveling at the naivete of her daughter in this matter of morals. She was glad, though, for she had always impressed upon her the difference between right and wrong and cautioned her to travel the straight and narrow in affairs of the emotions.

"Remember," she recalled saying to her a year or so back, when going steady was the rage of the teenage set, "you have only one body, and it's a very precious and sacred thing. It should be permitted to only one person beside yourself, and it is not his to own until you are one in the eyes of the law and of God." Gloria was very straitlaced in her thinking.

Lorene had understood and had never questioned her again regarding what was permissible or proper to do or not to do. Gloria had always had great faith in her daughter's judgment, and her last question, asked in all innocence, raised her faith just one notch higher.

"What do you mean she didn't go back to him?" Lorene asked. "You don't mean," she asked in surprise, "she had another boyfriend?"

"I'm afraid so, honey," Gloria replied.

"But how could she just hop from one boyfriend to another so quickly? And sleep with him too?" Lorene couldn't understand how or why a woman would do that. She understood having sex but not with a boyfriend. You had to be in love to do that.

"Don't you be her judge, darling. We don't know all the circumstances." Gloria had always been the tolerant member of the family, refusing to believe the worst in anyone until it was proven to her complete satisfaction. And even then she was always a stickler for believing the cause was almost as important as the result.

"But, Mother," Lorene questioned, "how can you say that? It's quite obvious what she did. In my book, Helen's nothing but a tramp."

"That's unfair of you, Lorene. I'm surprised to hear you say that."

"It's true, isn't it? If any of my friends slept around with more than one boy, that's what we would call her."

"I prefer not to think so. Let's just say she made a very bad mistake with the man. We have no proof there were anymore, and I don't think there were, not knowing Helen."

"One is bad enough," Lorene replied.

"Let's forget it for now, honey. How about us having some lunch and then baking a cake for supper?"

"Sounds fine to me. What shall we have?"

She pulled open the refrigerator, and the two of them scanned the contents.

"Lorene," Gloria said suddenly, "I think I just heard Joe put the mail in the slot. Run and catch him, honey. I have a letter to send out."

"Okay." She rushed out of the kitchen and into the front hall.

"The letter's on the foyer table," Gloria called after her.

She yelled back, "Got it!" Gloria heard the front door slam as Lorene ran out. When Lorene returned, Gloria had grilled cheese sandwiches waiting for them.

"What took so long?" Gloria asked as she put the plates on the table.

"By the time I got out the door he was three houses up the street. I guess one of the houses didn't get a delivery today. And then when I got there he remembered that he had forgotten to leave your magazine. Here it is." She dropped the *Woman's Home Companion* on the table and, lifting her knife and fork, started cutting into her sandwich. "At first he couldn't find the magazine and it took him a while to locate it. Then we talked for a few minutes."

"That doesn't sound like Joe, being so careless about a delivery," Gloria remarked.

"Oh, it wasn't Joe. I meant to tell you. We have a new mailman now."

"What happened to Joe? Did he say?"

"Nope. Just said to tell you he's the new man. His name is Frank, and he'll try to bring the mail earlier from now on as soon as he gets used to the route."

"Poor Joe," Gloria mumbled. "I guess they did fire him."

"What did you say?"

"Only that—" Her sentence was interrupted by the ring of the telephone. "Why must it always ring when I'm eating or busy?" Gloria asked.

"Want me to get it?"

"No, honey. Just finish your lunch."

There was a phone on the wall in the kitchen alongside the door to the dining room and close to the kitchen table. Gloria reached for the receiver with her left hand while her right cut the sandwich with her fork.

"Hello?" There was a slight pause. "Oh, hello, Gladys. How are you? We're fine here. Listen, can I call you back? I'm right in the middle of lunch. Oh, fine. I'll call you in a half hour or so. By the way, how's Eileen? Really? Oh, I'm sorry to hear that, but she'll most likely be all right. Lots of girls start to stain during the early part of their pregnancies. Of course I think she'll be okay. What does the doctor say? Well, then, if she stays in bed and takes those pills, she'll undoubtedly be back to normal in a week. Honestly," she laughed. "I think Ed was right. You are going to be an awful worrying grandma. Well, we'll see. I'll call you later. Goodbye, dear, and try not to worry too much."

"Eileen having trouble?" Lorene asked as her mother hung up the phone.

"Not really. I had the same difficulty when I was pregnant with you. It lasted a day or two and it was all over. You don't seem to be any the worse for it."

"I guess not. I hope Eileen is all right."

"I do too, honey. She and Peter want this baby desperately. They've been trying for five years to have it."

"Why is it that those people who don't seem to care can have ten or twelve or more but the ones who want children the most always have troubles?"

"Not always, Lorene."

"Well, too many times."

"I don't know, honey. I'm afraid no one can answer that except God himself."

"That's no answer, but I guess it's the only one. Life is a mystery, a riddle, filled with questions and answers forbidden to mortal man—"

Gloria interrupted her and poked her playfully. "You're not in philosophy class now, honey," she said, "so no lectures please."

"Class dismissed," Lorene answered with a laugh as she ate the last piece of her sandwich.

Chapter 12

The days rapidly melted into weeks for the young couple in love as they tried vainly to cherish each moment as long as possible, relinquishing it only reluctantly to grasp the next hour on their merry-go-round of time. Life for Lorene and Ray had been a succession of dates for the five weeks following their meeting. They swam in the blue Atlantic by day as well as by night; went boating and fishing in the waters of the sound; dined at hamburger havens and the finest French restaurants, though they were scarcely aware of the difference or of what they were consuming; danced to the melodies blasting from a jukebox and to the soft tunes from full-piece bands in nightclubs; and kissed beneath the light of the moon and stars. Each of them recognized a fervor within them that they believed could never have existed between any two people before. Throughout it all, Lorene persisted in eradicating the feelings of her father from her mind as she gloried in her newly found romance.

They had driven down Woodmere Boulevard, toward the docks, and were parked there, watching the reflections of the lights upon the water and the occasional light of a boat in the distance. They listened to the evening noises and the stillness of the people around them. Now and again the rustle of a taffeta skirt, a sigh, a brief girlish giggle, and the word *don't* in a tone suggesting cessation but encouraging progression interrupted the silence, but in the main, quiet reigned as a king.

Lorene and Ray sat side by side, his arm drawn tightly about her shoulders, looking out into the dark depths of the water.

"Lorene?" He said softly.

"Yes, Ray?" She tilted her head and rested it upon his shoulder.

"Happy?"

"Very." Somehow this did not seem to be the time for long replies.

"Know what?" he asked.

"No, what?"

"I kinda sorta like you." He turned to look at her.

"I'm glad," she answered.

"In fact, what I feel goes a bit deeper than that." He spoke slowly as if each word was difficult to say and he wasn't sure how to say what he wanted.

"How deep?"

"That's hard to answer. There never has been a machine to measure the depths of this emotion."

"Of love, you mean?" she whispered cautiously.

He answered quietly and simply, "Yes."

"I feel the same way, Ray."

"What shall we do about it?"

"You'll have to speak to Dad first."

"I'm a bit afraid to, after all you've told me about him."

"He's really not so bad. Besides, once he knows that you're serious, his whole attitude will change."

"I hope so," he answered.

"Have you told your folks yet?"

"Not really. I told Mother about you and that I loved you, but I'm afraid her reaction wasn't what I expected. Dad was completely different, though. Here, look at this." He drew a piece of paper from his pocket and handed it to her. It was folded in quarters, and as she opened it he switched on the car light so that she might read it. It was a letter from his father.

Dear Raymond,

The spontaneous and unrelenting fervor of your wooing is admirable. You will speak further with me about it, I am assured, and as usual, I shall speak my piece, present worldly and other problems before you for decision. The decision, as always, at this stage of your life should be made by you. I will not make if for you.

There are at least four parties, besides the lady and yourself, her mother, her father, your mother, and your father. And don't forget the young lady. All should be happy and satisfied. If one is not and the lady is willing, it presents a problem rather difficult to overcome and disrupts the harmony of the plan.

Assuming, but not conceding, that all interested parties are satisfied, do you and the young lady understand the problems that result and arise out of a commitment?

What have you to offer to Lorene, who comes, from what you have told me, from a very lovely home, who has tasted of the sweets of life and has not wanted for their comforts and necessities? You can offer her a splendid character that you possess, a healthy outlook on life, youth, ambition, a desire to make something of yourself, and the sound and solid roots from which you stem. What you offer is precious to a young lady. Not too many young men possess what you have to offer. Is Lorene willing to offer up the comforts of a home, the care and devotion of her lovely and very fine parents, to sacrifice temporarily or perhaps for a long time many of the luxuries that she now enjoys? Is she willing to travel along the highway of life with you, for good or bad, and together with you meet and conquer all the good and bad that you will encounter on this travel?

Is she willing to share with you the meager things in life that you can offer her now? Is she willing to sacrifice all the certain comforts and luxuries until you both make your way to the ultimate goal, whatever that may be, though it be other than riches and happiness? Does she understand that you cannot offer her, at this time, financial certainty?

And that you will have to hew your way for a long time? Does she understand your problems and your outlook on life? And is she willing to carry on with you? If she does and she understands all, then I do not and cannot, in all honesty, object. On the contrary, I consent. Lorene, from what you have told me, is a very fine, clean, honorable girl whose roots stem from fine and honorable parents. All this she offers you, a blessing in womankind.

One day, when all is adjusted between you, if that is the desire of both, I should like to sit down, just we three, and I would like to give you my studied ideas on how I would like to live were I young again. It might be interesting. There is much in life that sensible people can squeeze out of it, which, to the regret of many of us, we have failed to do. The world is beautiful, and with love it can be enjoyed, each moment of it, if we know just how life should be lived.

Pop

"That is beautiful," Lorene said as she folded the letter and handed it back to him. "We'll have to put that in our scrapbook. Your father must be a wonderful man. And he writes so beautifully."

"He's a great guy, and he loves to write. He fancies himself a philosopher."

"What did you mean about your mother's reaction to the news?" she asked. "Was she against it, like my father?"

"When I first told her, she seemed excited and happy about the prospect of my getting married. But then, as I told her more about you, your folks, who they were, and how your father objected, she changed. She seemed to feel that perhaps your father was correct, that it would be wisest for us to wait until I finished school before we committed ourselves."

"Then why did you ask me now?" Lorene asked.

"I thought it over and decided that I would like to get engaged now, to know that even though I'm away at school, you're all mine, waiting for me. I thought that in June I could get my degree in one hand and my wedding license in the other."

He leaned over to kiss her then, and he knew at once how much he wanted her. Nothing could stop him from marrying Lorene.

"That will be wonderful," she said as they broke apart for an instant. "And I have a marvelous idea. It's just past midnight. Mom and Dad will still be awake or just getting in; they were playing bridge tonight. Let's go home now, and I'll tell them all about us and ask Dad if it will be okay for you to speak with him tomorrow night."

"That idea sort of scares me. What if your father doesn't like the prospect of our engagement?"

"He'll be all right. Leave him to me."

"If that's what you want, honey, home we go." He started the car. "I guess you know your folks best."

When Lorene reached home, she found that her conclusions were correct. Her parents were reading in bed, not ready yet to turn out the lights and go to sleep yet too tired to concentrate fully on their books.

"Hi," Lorene said jollily as she entered. "How was the bridge game tonight?"

"Very nice," Gloria answered. "We had a few exciting hands, and your father and I made a small slam in spades—"

"Did you bid it?" Lorene asked. She had learned something of the game in the college student lounge during her free time just watching the students playing.

"Almost," Gloria replied. "We were playing the hand in five."

"Grossly underbid," Lorene teased.

"How come you're home so early, young lady?" Bob asked. He wanted to add, *Did you finally tire of your young man?* but he restrained himself and asked instead, "Didn't you have a good time?"

The past three weeks had been a living nightmare for Bob. He had done everything he knew to try to dissuade Lorene short of physically forcing her to stay home. Fortunately she had misinterpreted his actions as mere overprotectiveness and unjust prejudice, but he hadn't fooled Gloria. She knew that there was a much more important reason for his reaction, and he knew that he had forced her into a state of utter confusion. He felt badly for he wanted desperately to lead her out of this dilemma, and his only hesitations were in that he was afraid—not fearful of what he had done but of what her reaction to it would be. It was true that it was all in the past; it had happened so long ago it was almost hazy even to him. But after all these years he had kept it a secret from Gloria. He knew he should have confided in her years ago. Gloria was so straitlaced, so morally upright—would she understand? Would she forgive him? These were the questions to which he was afraid of hearing the answers, and as long as he was able he was determined to do everything he could to prevent her from finding out. He preferred leaving her in a state of confusion, even though it meant that her bitterness toward him was growing stronger. *No*, he had thought, *I can't tell her, not yet. Let her resent me temporarily. It's far more preferable than having her hate me forever.*

"I had a wonderful time, Dad. It's because I did that I'm home early."

"I don't follow you, honey. What you said doesn't make sense."

"I wanted to speak to you two before you went to sleep."

"Okay, honey, shoot." Bob closed his book and laid it on the bed next to him. He had a premonition, a bad feeling, about what was coming.

"Dad, Mother," she began. Now that the time was here she didn't know exactly how to express herself. The words of explanation she had drummed into her brain were suddenly gone.

"Yes, dear?" Gloria asked.

"Ray asked me to marry him. We want to become engaged." She blurted it out.

Bob was shocked. He was afraid this might happen eventually but didn't think it would happen yet. He had not allowed himself to believe the possibility. He had rationalized and deluded himself up until this very last minute. Now the dream bubble had burst. There was no longer any way to escape the truth.

"Do you love him, Lorene?" Gloria asked.

"Oh yes, Mom, very much."

"I think you do too," Gloria answered sympathetically.

"What makes you say that?"

"Because before, whenever you thought that you were in love, you always asked me the same question: 'Mother, what is love?' This time you didn't ask because you didn't have to. You knew the answer yourself."

"You're right. I do know the answer. We love each other very much. We hope to be married next June when Ray is graduated." She turned toward her father. "You're very quiet, Dad."

Bob's face had drained of all its color. "What do you expect me to say?" he asked.

"That you're happy for me," she replied.

"I can't say that, and you know it."

"Yes, you can, Dad. Your objection to Ray has been on the basis that you thought that I would be hurt, that he wasn't serious, and that I was foolish spending so much time with him. But you were wrong—that's proven now. Therefore, what objections can you have?"

"I don't like the boy."

"Dad, please! Oh, Mother," she appealed, "say something. He's so unreasonable."

Gloria remained silent for the moment, although her heart ached for her daughter. She realized that this was not the time to have it out with Bob.

"Lorene," Bob said, "sit down. Let's discuss this thing sensibly."

"All right, Dad." She sat on the edge of the bed awaiting his words anxiously. "But there's nothing to discuss," she added.

"Just what does this boy have to offer you?" He was down to

his final argument, and he had known, weak as it might be, that he would have to save it for just such an occasion as this.

"He's offering me himself, Dad. What else can he offer?" she asked.

"Nothing, and that's just my point. Why, you don't even know if this boy will be able to support you when he gets out of school, if he'll even have a job. You're not a poor girl who never had anything in her life. You're accustomed to certain luxuries, privileges that only money can buy. You don't realize what it is like not to have that money."

"Ray will go far; I know he will. He has the ambition, the brains, and the push to really go places," she answered. "I'll have as much as I have now, if not more, someday."

"Every young girl in love thinks that way," Bob countered. "Obviously, they're not all correct."

"Well, I am. I know Ray."

"Won't you even listen to reason?" he pleaded.

"What did you offer mother when you were married? You had just gotten out of school. You had no future."

"She's right, Bob," Gloria added. The time had come for her to interfere.

"Times were different then," he answered. "I was much more mature. I had been in the army and fought in the war."

"Love isn't changed by time," Gloria said.

"Am I to assume, then, that you are completely in favor of this match, Gloria, even knowing how I feel?"

"I told you I would have to be my own judge, Bob, and that's just what I'm doing. I made it a point to know Ray, to talk to him when he came to pick up Lorene. He seems to be a fine young man. His future is as bright as could be expected of most young men today. Offhand I have no objections."

"Hooray for you, Mother, and thanks!" Lorene was delighted

even though she knew that her mother's opinion had rarely been the deciding one, nor did it often sway her father. He was a strong man, staunchly set in his ways and predetermined in his actions.

"How could you, Gloria? How could you?" he asked. "To openly defy me before our daughter. We've always stood as a solid front before. And you didn't even listen to what other reasons I have."

"I can't fight an enemy I can't see," she replied simply. "Nor can I join forces with him. I'm standing my ground now because I believe I'm right. I'm taking my daughter's side because I can understand her and my heart aches along with hers. I'm not as devoid of emotion as you seem to be."

"That's unfair of you. Of all my faults you can never say I lacked understanding or feeling."

"Not until now, until one month ago when this boy entered our lives. Something changed in you then. You lost all sense of right and wrong, of fairness and honesty, and of sincerity. What brought this about I don't know, and frankly I don't care anymore. You've set your mind against Ray, and nothing that anyone says or does seems to change you at all. Your excuses are so obviously synthetic that you contradict yourself from day to day as your prime motivation makes you more panicky. If Lorene and Ray are in love, I'm all for it and my blessings go with them."

Bob dropped his head, not in shame or anger but in the realization that all that was spoken was the truth and to it he had no reply. He was against the union, and he was fabricating reasons why it should not take place. But it would be impossible for him to condone it.

"Dad, please say you'll talk to Ray tomorrow night. He's coming over to see you."

There was no answer as the man, fiercely fighting a hopeless battle, felt himself losing more and more ground until his back was up against the wall.

"Well, Bob?" Gloria asked.

"What would you have me tell him?" he asked.

"Just say yes, Dad. Just say yes," Lorene pleaded.

"I can't do that. I just can't."

"Why, Dad? Tell me why. Give me a good reason," Lorene pleaded.

Once again he had no answer, and in search of support he turned to his wife.

"Help me, Gloria," he begged. "Help me just this once because you believe in me, because I'm your husband. Trust me—this marriage will be no good. I can't explain now, but you must believe I know what I am talking about."

"No, I can't. Will it be no good because for some obscure reason you just don't like Ray? That's not reason enough. And as for any other reason, I've racked my brain in search of one, but it just doesn't exist. I can't help you this time. You're on your own."

"Won't you change your mind, Dad," Lorene asked. "Reconsider?"

He merely shook his head no.

"I'm going to my room. I can't stand this anymore. The way you act you'd think he had committed a murder or something and you were afraid to tell us," Lorene blurted out. "He's a fine, decent boy who loves me, and I love him and we'll be married."

"Lorene, honey, don't say that. Don't talk that way, please," he pleaded.

"Don't *honey* me, Dad. It doesn't fit in with your personality right now." She started for the door then turned for a final word. "And if you do continue to stand in our way, I'll hate you for the rest of my life."

"Lorene!" he shouted to her as she fled from the room.

"Is that what you want?" Gloria asked. "Do you want your daughter to hate you? Your son-in-law too? Would you make her your enemy without even giving her cause for a war?"

"God help me," he sobbed. "I don't know what to do."

"Lorene was partially right," Gloria added. "There is something you haven't told me, isn't there?"

"Yes." His answer was quiet and slow, almost inaudible.

"I can't imagine what it could possibly be. Has Ray done something? Surely there would be no reason to withhold any information of that sort."

"He hasn't done a thing," Bob answered. "Not a thing."

"Then what?"

Bob interrupted her question. "Give me some time to myself, Gloria." He requested. "I've got to think this thing through." He got out of bed and put on his robe.

"Where are you going?" she asked.

"To the den. I'll just sit there a while."

"Go ahead," she said. "And then come back and tell me what this is all about. I'll be waiting."

He kissed her gently on the forehead. "I must have given you some pretty rough weeks," he commented. "I'm sorry."

"Don't be sorry for me," she replied. "Only for Lorene."

Chapter 13

How long he sat in the brown leather den chair he did not remember. Time was of no concern. The dark room was silent, and he was weary, very weary. He knew the answer and understood what he had to do, regardless of the consequences. There was no alternative; Gloria had to be told the truth. He played with various alternative ways to relate the story, rejecting each one in turn. His dilemma weighed heavily upon him. He was tired, sleepy from pretense and from the pressure of the unavoidable revealing of his secret.

The silence in the dark room made him wearier, and he began to drift off slowly until consciousness was beyond his reach and he began to fall into the depths of blackness. Space surrounded him, drawing him deeper into its black web as the walls of reality drifted further and further away. He resented it as the web grew tighter about him, dragging him down into restless unconsciousness. He traveled willingly into another world, praying this burden of his would be left behind, if only for just a moment of peace.

"Why are you so slow?"

"Can't you see we are waiting for you?"

"Haven't you made up your mind yet?"

Three pair of eyes stared at him and conveyed these questions.

He looked downward. Couldn't they wait a minute? A deck of cards suddenly appeared before him. He reached for the ten of diamonds and discarded it. A hand darted out, picked up the trick, and retreated. The eyes leered at him again. He studied the cards in his hand, a king of diamonds and a queen and jack of hearts. The eyes grew impatient. The rest were his. He displayed his hand. The eyes blinked in agreement.

He was alone in a bright, noisy room. His three cards lay open on the floor. Suddenly strains of the wedding march could be heard. They grew louder and louder until even the walls rocked to their terrifying rhythm. The music caressed the sleeping cards and vibrated them to life. They followed the beat and twirled in a mad, frenzied dance. The cards spun round and round; the music grew faster and faster; his head began to throb and ache. Around and around they whirled. Over and over the music played. A bright light drew his eyes to a shimmering blade drifting toward his trio of cards. It dropped to the floor, its sharp metallic edges glimmering in the dim light. Darkness flooded the scene, and then light reappeared. The knife stabbed the body of the jack of hearts. The glittering surface of the blade was covered with the red of blood as were the hands of the king of diamonds. Darkness fell again, and the gray mass before his eyes slowly changed color until a sea of human blood lay before him.

Consciousness slapped him in the face. Leaping to its call, his shivering body ached with the horror he had witnessed. He reached for the lamp, welcoming the rays of reality that flooded the room.

"God help me," he said aloud. "What have I been thinking?" He massaged his damp brow roughly with his fingers.

"Gloria," he called, "I've got to talk to you." He started up the stairs. "I've got to talk to you now," he continued. "Right now. There's so much that I have to say."

CHAPTER

Chapter 14

When he entered the room, Gloria was sitting up in bed. Though her eyes were rimmed in red, an expression of relief was predominant.

"I'm so glad, Bob," she said. "So very happy."

"You may not be when you hear what I have to say," he replied. He sat down next to her and clasped her hands in his.

"Whatever you have to tell me, no matter what, I'll welcome it in preference to your silence. Now then," she asked, "what connection do you have with Ray?"

"What makes you say there is a connection?" he asked.

"There had to be. You obviously knew him, or of him, from somewhere, but what baffled me was that he didn't know you."

"He doesn't," Bob answered.

"Then what?"

"I think it's best if I start at the very beginning." He lit a cigarette and blew a thin line of smoke into the air before he began.

"I had just completed thirty days of basic training in the army and had received my first pass since I had enlisted. It was the end of September 1943, and I was in South Carolina. Greeben to be exact."

"But what has all this got to do with Ray?" Gloria asked.

"Don't interrupt me, honey, please. This is difficult enough. You don't have any idea how difficult."

"All right. Please continue," she said. "I'm sorry."

"I knew nothing about the town and no one in it, so I went to the USO. They were having a dance that night, and as usual a number of girls who worked there were present. I asked one of them to dance, and as we did she asked where I came from. I told her New York but that most of my family was from Rhode Island. I'll never forget her reply: 'You know,' she said, 'I never knew *damn Yankee* was two words until I was fifteen years old.'

"I was a silly, hotheaded young kid then, just about as old as Lorene is now, and I got angry, so angry that I walked out of the place immediately. I was insulted."

Gloria was becoming impatient. She could not, as yet, see any connection, and it took all of her willpower to check her questions and allow him to continue.

"The following weekend I got another pass and found myself at a bar to get a drink. When I walked in, there was this girl I had met the week before sitting with a soldier and another girl. I figured the soldier was her date and that the extra girl was lonesome, so I went over to them. As it turned out, the USO girl was with her sister and brother-in-law. Well, we got to talking and we struck up a friendship. She apologized for her remark the week before; she didn't realize it would offend me. Her name was Allison, Allison Zell, and she had an apartment in town with a girlfriend. Her folks lived on a cotton plantation about seventy miles away. We spent the evening together and subsequent ones after that. We kissed and hugged and petted a lot, but we weren't intimate. She was a wonderful girl, simple and sweet, and before we realized it we had become steady dates. Several times we went by bus out to her parents' home to spend weekends there. Her folks were lovely people and wonderful to me. They knew that I liked to eat roasted rabbit, so they always prepared it for me. I shed my uniform and wore her brother's clothes. When the chilly October nights set in, we'd all sit in the living room in front of a big roaring fireplace. One night we sat there for a few hours after her mother and dad had retired, and she told me that she cared for me quite a lot. It was that night she slipped into my room and spent the rest of the evening with me. It was my first time with Allison and her first time with anyone."

Gloria could contain herself no longer. "But what has all of this to do with Ray?" she asked.

"This is all part of the background of my story," he explained. "It's important for you to understand what sort of person Allison was."

"Wait a minute, Bob," Gloria said as the importance of his story was becoming clear to her. "Isn't Ray's mother's name Allison?"

"Yes, it is."

"Then your objection has to do with Ray's mother, not Ray himself? Do you feel awkward?" She hoped that was the reason, but deep inside her gut told her it was not. "Do you feel uncomfortable because of how well you two knew each other? Is that it?"

"No, that isn't the whole thing. Please let me finish, Gloria. It will all be clear soon enough."

"All right," she said. "I'm sorry I interrupted."

"From then on we continued to have affairs whenever we met until a short time later when I was transferred to a new camp in Texas," Bob continued. "I wrote to Allison, received no reply, and wrote again. When no answer came I wrote to her sister.

"She answered my letter and explained that Allison, and Allison's folks, had thought that I would marry her, but since I had left without saying anything and gave her no reason to think that I loved her. she was hurt and didn't want to be in contact with me anymore."

"Did you love her, Bob? You tried to stay in touch with her, so she must have meant something to you."

"No, not really. I cared for her quite a bit but not enough to marry her. Besides, I was the footloose and fancy-free Casanova at that time, all of nineteen or twenty. I wasn't ready to settle down."

"I see. Please continue," she said.

"Well, it seems, according to her sister's letter, that Allison was so disappointed that when she met a GI shortly after I left who wanted to marry her, she accepted. He was going to Aerial Gunnery School in Texas, and Allison was planning to go there to marry him when he graduated. I heard no more about her until one night I was paged while in my barracks and told that a lady wanted to see me. It was Allison. She had married George Bishop the day before, and he had been shipped overseas that next morning."

"George Bishop? That's Ray's father, isn't it?"

"Yes."

"What was she doing at your base?" Gloria asked.

"She was on her way back home and decided to stop off to say hello to me before she left."

"When was this?" Gloria asked.

"April of 1944."

"But why did she want to see you?"

"Because, she said, she still loved me."

"How sad for her." Gloria was sympathetic. "Did she leave for home after seeing you?"

"No, as a matter of fact she spent one week with me," he answered.

"One week! But she was married!" Gloria exclaimed in shock. "Why would you do such a thing? You weren't in love with her."

"Explanations are difficult now, Gloria." He wrung his hand in a futile attempt to express himself. "Maybe it was because I did care for her or because I knew she loved me despite marrying someone else and my own manly pride was too great. I was flattered. Maybe it was because we were just kids or because the war was on and we lived for each moment. Who knows why? And truthfully the why isn't important anymore, only what happened."

"The why isn't important? Isn't important?" Gloria emphasized the words. She was stunned and almost speechless. "Your excuses don't hold water," she continued. "I can't believe you had absolutely no morals. She was married, and you were leading her on. It was despicable. You let your stiff cock and your ego rule your head. Shame on you. Surely there were plenty of single girls available"

"Please, Gloria." Bob was stunned with the vehemence of her attack. "I realize that this must be a shock to you and quite painful, but I have to tell it to you now. Why do you think I waited so long before I did? I didn't want you to know this for anything in the world. I wanted to protect you as long as I could from something that I felt was unnecessary for you to learn. I feared the reaction you would have. I was afraid you would want nothing to do with me. But now you know. You had to know. I am risking your love and understanding. I am praying that your love for me will override your disillusionment and your possible hatred of me. I have a lot at stake, Gloria, and I'm not a gambling man. I know how wrong I was. I've thought of it many times. But I did what I did; I can't change it now. Now I must deal with the ramifications of what I did, and I need you to help me, to stand beside me."

"You'd better continue, Bob. I gather that the story doesn't end here," she said unemotionally, staring off into space as she did so. She dreaded what she was about to hear.

"Yes, there is more to the story. Allison went home at the end of the week, and a short time later I was transferred to a base in Wisconsin. One night I got a telephone call from her. She was calling from her folks' home in South Carolina, and she was crying. She asked me if it would be all right if she came to see me. I said it was okay with me but asked what her mother would say, especially since she was married? She said, 'I'll let you talk to Momma.' Well, I told her mother that I'd like to see Allison but only if it was with her consent. She said it was okay with her. Naturally I was surprised, but who was I to complain, especially if it was okay with Momma?"

"But didn't her mother realize what would happen when you were together? Why you were going to see each other? That is, what you would do?" Gloria could not imagine a mother giving her permission for her married daughter to have an affair with another man. "The whole thing doesn't make sense," she added. "There has to be more to this story."

Bob continued. "Afterward, I realized that Allison's mother must have hoped that I would ask Allison to divorce her husband and marry me. But it didn't occur to me at the time, and I wouldn't have asked her even if I had thought of it because I didn't want to marry her and I wasn't ready to marry."

"It still doesn't make sense," Gloria said. "Why would her mother want her to get a divorce? Were you should a great catch? Why would she want her to marry you?"

"Let me finish, and it will all become clear. At the time I didn't understand it either. When Allison arrived, I had everything ready. I had rented an apartment under the name of Mr. and Mrs. Robert Ruthers because Allison had told me she wanted to stay for a while. You see, I was able to get all the night passes I wanted from a close friend of mine who was in charge of details and passes. So I slept in town, and my friend called me if something came up that I had to be back for. I had finished basic training but, being in the army air force, we were still training and getting flying time. We knew we were due to go overseas at any time and were waiting to be assigned."

"Please, stop for a minute," Gloria requested. "I'm so shocked at this point that I have to have a second before I hear anymore. I always knew that you had been a man about town before we were married, and when we were engaged I was glad. I was a virgin and inexperienced. I was happy that you would know what to do. I wanted you to teach me, which you did. And you told me that you were happy that I had not been with anyone else. I was happy that you had had sexual experiences. But this—this is beyond my wildest expectations. This isn't the story of a GI who wanted to have sex." Her brow wrinkled a bit and her eyes stared blankly at him as she spoke. "This is a boy who took it from a good girl, who continued to take her love and give sex in return." She added, "Even though she was married to someone else. And for what? Why? There were girls aplenty looking for a handsome young soldier without resorting to a girl, a married woman, whose true love he knew he could never return, whose love for him he knew was greater than her love for her husband. Why, Bob? Why?" she pleaded for an answer.

"I can't answer that, Gloria. I have no answer. But let me finish, please. You're only making it harder for me."

"There's more? "she exclaimed. "What more can there be? Did she get a divorce? Did you marry her?"

"No, nothing like that," Bob answered. "I had been spending most nights there for a while. One night we were lying in bed making plans for the evening. She didn't seem too keen about doing anything, and jokingly I said, 'What's the matter Allison? You're certainly getting lazy and fat too. You have to stop lying around all day.'

"She looked at me quite surprised and said, 'Don't you know why I'm lazy and fat?'

"Then it dawned on me. I asked her, 'Are you pregnant?'

"She said, 'It's about time you realized it.'"

Gloria gasped.

"If you feel shocked now, Gloria, you can imagine how I felt. I nearly fell off of the bed. We talked about it then, and it was evident that we had a problem."

Now the situation was clear to Gloria. She tried to speak and then slowly pushed out the words. "Do you mean that—that Ray is your …" She could not continue any further. She felt a lump rising in her throat.

"That was the problem, Gloria. Allison thought I must have been the father. That was why she was hoping I would marry her. But there was no proof. Her husband, George, could have been the father too. She had spent one night with George and one week with me. Either one of us could be the father. We discussed it, and I told her that since she was married it was best if she returned home and resumed her married life. I explained to her, again, that I was not going to marry her."

Gloria started to cry.

Bob reached out for her and grasped her shoulders. "Honey, please don't cry. You see, we don't know. We can't know. Ray may not be my—"

Gloria interrupted, "Your son." Quietly, she said, "Now I understand why Momma wanted Allison to be with you. They both thought you were the father and that, knowing that, you would marry her. Did you feel any pangs of responsibility?"

"No. Once again, he may be mine, but then again he may not."

"What happened after that, Bob?" She felt there might be more to the story.

"Nothing much. Allison went home the next day. We wrote occasionally, and shortly after I was shipped overseas. While I was in the Philippines I got one letter from her with a picture of the baby boy enclosed. I never heard from her again."

"When you knew the baby might be yours, why didn't you ask her to marry you?"

"Why? I might not have been the father. Why should I have married her when I didn't love her, especially since she was already married and had a husband who would believe the child to be his and raise him as his son?"

"But she was married to a man she didn't love," she argued.

"Not so. She told me that George was a great guy for whom she had good feelings, though not the kind of love she had for me. I'm sure she's had a happy life with him. But that's not the point now, Gloria. That's all in the past. The right or wrong of my actions has nothing to do with the situation at hand. Can't you see that we must stop this pending marriage? How can we let them marry knowing that they may be blood relations?"

"I guess Allison is sure they are," Gloria said.

"Because of our names, you mean." It was clear that Bob had realized that before. "Yes, she named her baby Raymond Ryan, obviously after Robert Ruthers. What can we do, Gloria? What can we do?" Bob pleaded for an answer. "I've done everything I know of or could think of to stop it. You can see now that we have to do more than try. We must succeed."

"Why didn't you tell me all this sooner, Bob? As soon as you knew who Ray was, you should have told me. At least I would have understood why you reacted the way you did."

"At first I felt there was no need to, that nothing would come of their chance meeting except a date or two. Then as things became more serious I was hoping against hope that it would all blow over and be nothing more than infatuation. I was willing to risk your resentment of me temporarily, hoping you would write it off as a father unwilling to relinquish his daughter and forget it in time. But when things reached a climax tonight, I knew you had to be told."

"And all these years, didn't you ever wonder if you had a son somewhere?" she asked.

"I didn't let myself think about it, and if I did I convinced myself that the boy was George's, not mine. I could do that all these years, up until now when I was forced to admit the possibility to myself and now to you."

"What do you think should be done?"

He ignored the question and asked his own. "Do you hate me now, Gloria, for what I did and for having deceived you all these years?"

"I don't hate you, Bob. I don't hate you at all. I am terribly hurt and I'm disappointed because you chose to conceal it from me all these years. However, it's over and done and nothing can change it. You've been my husband for all these years, and they have been good years filled with joy and love. This was something that happened before we were married, before you knew I existed. I love you, but I feel that I have seen a side of you that I didn't know existed and I don't like what I see.. You were self-serving and without feeling for another human being who you cared for. I cannot believe you could have walked away from the situation without a second thought. I will always love you, but I can never forgive you."

"Did I tell you recently how very much I love you, darling?" he said tenderly. "And how much I need you?"

"It's always nice to hear, but it doesn't change things."

"I love you, Mrs. Ruthers, and I never loved another."

"Thank you. That was very sweet of you, but we've a greater problem on hand than your love for me."

"I don't know what to do, Gloria. I haven't the faintest idea."

"I wonder if Allison knows who Lorene is?" she questioned.

"She might suspect. Ray must have told her about Lorene and us too, I suppose."

"Then she would be as set against this as we are. She may be of some help," Gloria suggested.

"I don't see how. Her pleas to Ray would have fallen on deaf ears as did mine to Lorene."

"There's only one thing that I can suggest now. But I'd really like to think this through."

"What were you thinking?" he asked.

"You'll have to tell Lorene, just as you told me."

Bob was startled. The idea hadn't occurred to him, and he didn't like it. The last thing he wanted was for Lorene to know.

"If you can't tell her," Gloria continued, "perhaps I can. It would be easier for me."

"No, definitely not!" Bob was emphatic. "Do you realize what it would mean? She would hate me, not only for what I did in the past but for what I am doing to her life now. She couldn't understand; she's too young. To her I'm her father, nothing else. Can a girl her age and from her background realize that her father was once young, had emotions, desires, affairs? No, I won't do it. I won't risk her love, her respect. There must be another way."

"You were willing to risk my love," Gloria said softly. "Perhaps she will understand."

"That was different. You're older and more mature, and you knew me when I was much younger. You remember the passions of youth. A wife hopefully can understand and forgive her husband the sins of his past, but not a daughter. She can't understand and forgive her father. And remember, I didn't risk telling you until the very end, until the last moment. I won't ever consider telling Lorene, not unless all else fails me."

"I can see no other alternative," Gloria said. "But," she added, "maybe there's someone else who can help."

"Who?" he asked anxiously.

"Allison"

"Do you mean that you think I should see her? After all these years?"

"I think it's a necessity. Her son is involved too—don't forget."

"Will you come with me?" he asked.

"No, this is something for the two of you to discuss alone. She might be embarrassed to know that I know the whole story. Actually, meeting you again may be very difficult for her considering how she felt about you. And, don't forget, since she believes that you are the father of her son, the meeting could be that much more difficult. I'm sure she never expected to see or meet you again. And what about you, Bob? How will you feel seeing her again? You did have feelings for her back then. Will they be renewed?"

"Don't be silly. I have no feelings for her today," he answered. "I don't particularly care to see her after all these years, and I imagine she will feel the same way. It will bring back some memories that are best forgotten. It will be very awkward. Of course, we are assuming that she will be willing to meet with me."

"Call her tomorrow, Bob, the sooner the better. I'm sure she will meet with you."

"There's no other way, I suppose."

"None," she said, "unless you tell Lorene."

"I'll call her in the morning. I'll try to meet her for lunch. What do you think?"

"That's a good idea. You want a relaxed atmosphere. She lives in New Jersey. Do you think she'll come into the city?"

"I hope so. Her town is just over the bridge, so getting into the city should be no problem." He switched off the light and lay down. His mind did not feel as heavy now that he had told Gloria. A weight had been lifted off of him.

CHAPTER

Chapter 15

Bob Ruthers wove his way through the crowded Long Island section of the Pennsylvania Railroad Station and walked rapidly through the underground maze of tunnels, past department stores, past his usual stop for a second breakfast of coffee and doughnuts at a favorite stand, and on to the subway. He waited patiently on the jammed platform until his train arrived, and then, finding no vacant seats, he was forced to stand all the way downtown. He automatically hung onto a strap, seeing and hearing nothing, and managed to find his way off at the proper station only through an automatic reflex that years of the self-same travel had developed.

He reached the company building early that morning, and going directly to his office he closed the door behind him and stood for a moment with his back against it while he consciously inhaled the musty odor created by a closed office overnight. It was a good-sized office with a large window overlooking the busy New York City street below. The room was furnished tastefully with a desk, some bookcases (one of which housed a fully equipped bar), an easy chair, a loveseat, and a cocktail table. The company was an engineering firm specializing in pneumatic conveying systems, and Bob was one of its vice presidents. The prospect of what was to come was not pleasant for him. He dreaded the thought of rekindling the ashes of the past, of meeting a woman who was now, despite memories, a mere stranger to him. He wondered fleetingly how she would look and act. He sat down behind his executive desk and pulled out the New Jersey telephone directory for the city of Clinton. He turned the pages until he reached the B's. His forefinger ran quickly over the names: Billera, Binder, Bing. He skipped a number of rows and started again: Bird, Birdsall, Bischof … Bishop. George Bishop, 30 Val Park Road. *That's it*, he thought. He picked up a pencil and circled the phone number.

The clock on his desk read five minutes past nine when he contacted the company's switchboard operator to put the call through. With his free hand he lit a cigarette as he sat waiting, only to grind it out rapidly when he heard the phone begin to ring on the other end. For a moment he was tempted to hang up, to forget the whole thing, but he knew that that wasn't the solution. The telephone rang for the third time and a sense of relief passed through him. *Maybe she's not home*, he thought. *Maybe she's not home.*

The telephone on the mahogany knee hole desk in the living room rang for the fourth time. The instrument seemed very much in place in this small room furnished more like a den than a parlor. A worn, amber-colored Louis XIV couch stood against the wall opposite the desk flanked by two wooden bookcases that were filled mainly with pocket edition detective stories. In addition there were volumes dealing with philosophy, religion, law, and psychology. Against the wall to the left of these pieces were twin brown-velvet barrel chairs, and the space between them was filled with a round, lightwood cocktail table. An archway adjoining the jangling telephone led to the dining room, which had a rear door that opened into the backyard, where Allison was busily hanging up her wash on a spiral clothesline. It wasn't until the fifth ring that she heard the phone, and then she rapidly made her way back into the house, brushing a lock of blond hair from her eyes as she did. Despite the toll that the years had taken, she remained a very pretty woman—a bit stouter, perhaps, with the facial lines of youth replaced by those of maturity, but nonetheless attractive even in her plaid wrap-around housedress.

She rushed through the dining room into the parlor, and as she lifted the receiver on the sixth ring she wondered who would be calling her so early.

"Hello?" she questioned.

"I'd like to speak to Mrs. George Bishop, please," the man's voice on the other end requested.

"This is Mrs. Bishop. Who is this?" she asked.

`"Allison? Is that you?" he asked.

"Who is this?" she replied. "How do you know me?" She was puzzled. The voice sounded familiar, but she couldn't place it.

"This is Bob, Allison. Bob Ruthers."

There was dead silence on Allison's end.

"Allison, are you there?" Bob asked.

"Yes," she replied slowly. "I am just a bit surprised. It's been so long, so very long."

"I know," he said. "But I had to call you. I just had to call you. I suppose you can guess why."

"I have a good idea," she replied. "I suspected Lorene was your daughter after Ray told me her last name. *Ruthers* isn't that common a name. But it was only a suspicion; it could have been someone else. How did you know Ray was my son? Did you remember my married name? There are loads of Bishops around."

"It was his name," Bob replied. "The double R's together with Bishop. And you did tell me his name years ago after he was born."

"Oh!" she exclaimed. "All these years, Bob, you never contacted me. You never cared how my son was doing or how I was doing. I thought you loved me. We were both in love. I couldn't understand why you didn't care whether I was happy or how my life was going. After I sent you a picture of the baby, I never heard from you again. I had no idea where you were or how to reach you after you were discharged. But for me, I want you to know that I am very happy. George is a wonderful man. He's a great husband and a fantastic father. I don't want anything to ruin that."

"I am happy for you, Allison. I only wanted the best for you. I agree—I was very remiss. I didn't act properly. I should have contacted you. But that's in the past. Right now we have a problem, and that's why I want to talk with you. I want to discuss the situation with you. There's so much to decide as to what to do. How can we handle the problem? Will you meet me for lunch today?"

"Today?" she questioned.

"The sooner the better," he answered.

"Yes, I'll meet you. Where?" she asked.

"Can you come into the city?"

"Yes, if you want."

"There's a Chinese restaurant on Seventh Avenue that I eat in often. It's quiet there, and we won't be disturbed. Is that all right with you?"

"That sounds fine. What's the name of the place?" she asked as she reached for a pencil and paper.

"It's Lotus Gardens. L-O-T-U-S," he spelled, "Gardens. It's on Seventh Avenue, I believe between Fifty-First and Fifty-Second Streets. Maybe Fiftieth and Fifty-First Streets. But you can't miss it. It's on the east side of the street."

"I'll be there, "she replied. "Twelve thirty okay?"

"Fine, I'll see you then."

"Goodbye, Bob."

"Goodbye, Allison."

He hung up the receiver first, but she held it until she heard the click on his end. Then she slowly placed the handle back in its cradle. Somehow she had expected this. She knew that something had to be done. She thought it ironic that she had loved Bob and thought he had loved her, and now their children were in love. *Must be genetic*, she mused, and she giggled at the thought. She looked at the clock—9:15. She knew she had better hurry if she expected to finish all her housework in time to meet Bob. She went back to her chores reluctantly, accomplishing them automatically, her mind far away in the distant past. She wondered what Bob looked like now. *Is he still as handsome? Does he still have his hair? Does he have the middle-age pouch, or is he in good shape? Well, I'll soon find out*, she thought.

When it came time to dress, she surveyed her closet for the proper outfit to wear. She chose carefully, wanting to make the proper impression especially since she knew from Ray of the success Bob had had. Ray had told her of the Ruthers' lovely house in the Five Towns area on Long Island, their nice car, and the cabana they had at the beach. She did not want to appear anything but prosperous herself. She was not poor—far from it. George made a good living, and they lived a wonderful middle-class life. They could afford just about anything they wanted or needed, and they were happy. Finally, she selected her newest daytime cotton dress. It was a simple, collarless black-and-white-print frock with small buttons to the waist and a wide, black belt gathering in a half-circle skirt. The sleeves were capped and had a solid black facing all around. She slipped the dress on and looked at her reflection in the mirror. *Not bad*, she thought, *not bad at all*. On her feet she wore a pair of black leather pumps. She placed a rope of white beads around her neck and put on the matching earrings. She applied her makeup sparingly, just a little powder and a light shade of lipstick. At 11:45, she left the house and unconsciously began to walk faster and faster. She was anxious to meet Bob again.

Chapter 16

Helen's work seemed slower and more inadequate than ever to Gloria this morning, though her trips to the bathroom were fewer and less lengthy than they had been for the past week. Gloria had been intending to speak with her again to inquire as to how she felt, but her own preoccupation on this particular day was distracting enough to drive Helen and her problems from her mind. She had been reading a magazine all morning, nervously waiting for the phone to ring. At the slightest sound she sat erect, on the edge of her chair, hoping that perhaps it was the telephone. The instrument, annoyingly enough, had not been still all morning. It had rung four times in the last hour. Lorene had received a call, which lasted for twenty minutes despite Gloria's constant prodding to leave the line free because she expected an important call from Bob. Mrs. Winters had called to remind Gloria of the date of the first meeting of the choral group after its summer disbandment, and Helen had been the recipient once from some woman who wanted her to serve a dinner for sixteen people a week from Saturday night for some charity organization. The final call had turned out to be a wrong number.

Why doesn't he call me? Gloria questioned herself. *He knows*

I'm anxious to find out whether he's meeting Allison today. She picked up her magazine and tried unsuccessfully once again to concentrate on its printed page. *Perhaps,* she reasoned, *he's waiting to call me after he sees her so he'll have something to tell me. That must be it.* She flipped the pages of the magazine until her eyes fell on the title "A Box of Matches." *Sounds fascinating,* she thought. *I'll read this.*

For a few minutes she was completely absorbed in the story, which turned out to be a mystery. She was so involved that when Helen entered the room, she took no notice of her.

"Mrs. Ruthers," Helen called softly, "I think I'll get my lunch now."

"Of course, Helen, go right ahead," Gloria answered without looking up.

Helen started for the door, walking slowly and slightly stooped.

"By the way," Gloria called, looking up from the magazine, "I meant to ask you before. How do you feel now?"

"Pretty good today, ma'am. I slept last night for the first time in a while." She smiled a wide smile, revealing pearly white teeth. "You sure do need your sleep."

"Why weren't you sleeping?" Now Gloria put the magazine down on her knees with the pages opened.

"Well, I was throwin' up, but I ain't throwin' up anymore. And I feels good."

"I'm happy to hear that. You know that many women have terrible bouts of nausea at the beginning of their pregnancies," Gloria said. "I'm glad to hear your pregnancy is going well now. You must be thrilled, especially after having lost your last baby."

"Maybe it was the pills the doctor give me," Helen answered.

"Well, it doesn't make much difference," Gloria replied. "The important thing is that you're fine now."

"I guess so, ma'am. I'm happy 'bout that."

Gloria watched Helen's bulky form as she walked into the kitchen and thought, *What will become of that baby?* Then, shaking her head as if to throw loose the idea, she resumed reading.

It was four o'clock when Gloria tried calling Bob at the office for the third time. Her first and second attempts had been at two and three o'clock. She didn't want to call earlier because she didn't know how long Bob and Allison's lunch would last, if indeed they did get together. Each time she called, after being connected to Bob's office, she received the same reply.

"I'm sorry, Mrs. Ruthers," Bob's secretary answered sweetly. "Mr. Ruthers isn't back from lunch yet, and he left no word as to when to expect him."

"Thank you," Gloria replied each time. "Would you ask him to call me as soon as he returns?"

"Of course, Mrs. Ruthers. I'll see to it that he gets the message as soon as he comes in."

Gloria put the receiver back in its cradle slowly. *What in the world could be keeping him? Why haven't I heard from him? Doesn't he know how anxious I am?* All these questions kept running through her mind. *I won't call again*, she thought. *I won't be a pest. He'll call me soon, I'll just wait.*

Having completed her fourth magazine story and being terribly disappointed in its plot and writing style, she turned to a novel she had selected from the lending library. "*Race of Time* by George Comcroft," she read aloud, and she figured that it must be good because it was on *The New York Times* best-seller list. *Not that I always agree with their reviews*, she thought, *but I'll give it a try.*

She settled herself comfortably, a box of chocolates and a pack of Chesterfields beside her, and began to read. The book seemed excellent, justifying the reviews. Right from the opening lines— "The woman lay nude on the bed perspiring profusely from the mid-summer heat. Starting at the base of her throat, the sweat droplets raced each other as they rolled past her firmly rounded breasts and on toward her navel"—it demanded her attention and forced her to read on in anticipation of what was to come. She was so enthralled with the novel that she was startled when the telephone rang. Quickly she reached for the receiver eager to hear from Bob.

"Hello? Oh, Gladys, I thought you were Bob. I've been expecting him to call. What is it? You sound as if you're crying. What? Oh, Gladys, I am sorry, truly sorry. When did she lose the baby? This morning? How does she feel? Well, I realize she must be rather blue mentally, but is she all right? That's good, and it's something to be thankful for. Yes, I know how much she wanted it. And I know how much you looked forward to being a grandmother. If it's any consolation, at least she can have another someday. Please send her my best wishes and tell her I'm so very sorry to hear the news. What? Oh, well, I won't keep you since Ed's there now. Thanks for calling, and telling me and if there's anything I can do. All right, Gladys, goodbye, and try to pull yourself together."

She put the receiver back slowly, shaking her head in sorrow for Eileen, and returned to her book and became so deeply engrossed in it once again that, when Helen appeared and asked, "What you planning for supper, Mrs. Ruthers,? Should I put it up?" she was completely startled.

"What?" Gloria put the book down and looked at Helen. "What time is it?"

"Twenty to six, Mrs. Ruthers, and your supper won't be done if it don't get up now."

"Twenty to six? I can't believe it. I'll be right in to show you what to prepare, and then I must get ready to go to the station to pick up Mr. Ruthers."

Helen disappeared back into the kitchen, and Gloria, running her fingers through her hair, worried about what had happened to Bob and why he hadn't called.

Chapter 17

Bob had arrived at the restaurant early and, with the help of the distinguished Chinese manager, George Leto, chose a secluded table for two in the rear. The place was dimly lit and quite fashionable in its design. A mahogany bar ran the length of the room on the right, and the mirrors lining the wall behind it reflected the interior in all its Oriental splendor. The remaining sections of the room were filled with round tables and rectangular booths, all upholstered in a bright persimmon. Along the walls, from chair rail to ceiling, were hand-painted murals depicting Chinese life and customs. Flanking the entrance from floor to ceiling were two round posts, papered in a black-and-white marbleized pattern, making them look like two gigantic marble guards. The entire scene was extremely pleasing to the eye and conducive to enjoying some of the best and most unusual Oriental dishes in New York City. Bob felt comfortable here, out of the sweltering August heat of the city and breathing cool, fresh air blown abundantly throughout the room. He lit a cigarette and ordered a martini to kill some time and to assist in bolstering his nerves. When it arrived he toyed with it nervously for a few minutes and then downed it quickly in two gulps. The large clock on the wall above the cashier's counter showed that it was just twelve thirty. He hoped that Allison would not be too late. One martini later she was there, standing in the doorway looking around for him. He would have known her anywhere. The years had changed her very little, and seeing her stirred up memories of the past—how much he had loved her and how much they had loved each other. It was not until she came closer, with the aid of the waiter George, who had asked if she was the lady Mr. Ruthers was expecting, that he saw the difference. Twenty-four more years of life, work, and worry had etched themselves deeply into her face. He wondered if she was thinking the same thing about him as he rose to greet her.

"Hello, Allison," he said softly, reaching out to grasp her hand.

"Bob," she replied quietly as he gently squeezed her fingers in his.

"Sit down, please," he said.

She slid into the booth facing him and placed her pocketbook on the seat next to her.

"Would you like a cocktail before lunch?" Bob asked.

"That sounds nice," she answered. She removed her gloves and placed them neatly over her bag. Bob couldn't help observing her unmanicured nails, a bit roughened from work. *So unlike Gloria's*, he thought.

"What will you have?" he asked as the waiter appeared.

"A whiskey sour will be fine."

"I'll have another martini," he added.

"You're looking very well," Allison said as the waiter disappeared in the direction of the bar. "The years have been good to you."

"You haven't changed much," Bob said. "I'd have known you anywhere."

"Things have been pretty good with me." She reached into her pocketbook and withdrew a handkerchief to blow her nose gently. "I've got a summer cold that I just can't seem to shake," she explained.

"I'm sorry to hear that. What have you been taking for it?" he asked solicitously, knowing that he was just stalling for time, hesitant to start the conversation. It seemed that there would be small talk until one of them was ready to broach the subject.

The chit-chatting continued, covering the advantages of certain nose drops over others throughout the soup course; the advisability of using specialists with the egg roll; medical experiences of the past with the chop suey; and finally, remembrances with the dessert. The after-dinner cigarette brought with it a recap of the past twenty years, and as they finally reached the present, the reality of the purpose for their meeting was brought into focus. Bob was the one to bring up the subject.

"Allison, I asked you to meet with me so we could discuss the situation we have with the children. What do you think we should do?" Bob asked. "We can't let them go ahead with their plans. They may be …" He found it difficult to say.

"They may be related," she said, finishing his sentence. "I don't know what to do," she replied truthfully. "When I realized who Lorene was, and when I found out how serious Ray was about her, I tried everything that I knew to dissuade him. I told him he should wait until he finished school, until he had a job, and until Lorene was older. She's only eighteen, isn't she?"

Bob nodded. Only eighteen, and she was unknowingly facing one of the greatest crises in her life.

"I reasoned," she continued. "I argued and I begged. But he loves her, deeply, and nothing I could say would change that. I know how he feels, Bob. I felt the same way." She reached for her teacup, took a sip, and then added, "We felt the same way."

Bob did not want to get into a discussion of what had happened years ago, so he ignored her final statement.

"I tried too. God knows how I've tried. But nothing helped. I used the same arguments that you did." He shook his head silently and lit another cigarette. "What about George?" he asked as he exhaled his first puff of smoke.

"George?" she was confused.

"Does he know?" Bob asked. "About us?"

Allison was shocked. "Know? Of course not, and I'll never tell him." She was horrified at the thought. "George is a wonderful man. He has been a fabulous father and a more than stupendous husband. I have had a great life with him. Ray is his son, and even a suggestion of anything else would kill him. I refuse to have him learn of any of this. Besides, we don't really know, do we? George could easily have been Ray's father."

"I told Gloria," Bob said with a pause, "everything. I felt I had to."

Allison stared at him unbelievingly and then, closing her eyes, dropped her head toward her lap. Without looking up, she asked, "You told her we were in love?"

Bob repeated, "I told her everything. She understood, Allison. She understood perfectly, and she holds no ill feelings. I had to tell her. You can understand that, can't you? I couldn't justify my objections any other way. She had to know why I felt so strongly. She had to know so that she could help me. I felt we had to have a united front with Lorene."

Allison's face revealed her feeling. She was hurt and shocked. "How could you tell her how much in love we were? Wasn't that hurtful? She must hate me." Allison was still looking down.

"Hate you? Of course not. She understood. If she was angry with anyone, it was me. She thought my actions were despicable." Bob deliberately neglected to say that he never told Gloria that he had been in love with Allison. He reached across the table for her hand, but she withdrew it quickly and placed it in her lap, where she wrung her handkerchief into a thin, twisted rope.

"Then she pities me, feels sorry for me."

`"No, no, she doesn't. You don't know Gloria. She's a wonderful person full of sympathy and understanding."

"Well, you be sure to tell her that I am just fine. Tell her that I have had a good life and things turned out very well for me. I would not change a thing. It's okay that you told Gloria, but I won't tell George and I don't want him to find out. I won't destroy his life." She raised her eyes to meet Bob's, revealing a well of dampness in each. "And," she added emphatically, "*no one* is going to tell him."

"I think I understand," he said quietly.

"No, you don't. You couldn't. What happened with us is a thing of the past as far as your wife is concerned. But to George, it would not be the past; it would be the present. Every time he looked at our son, he would wonder. He would remember the great lie I withheld from him. He thinks I've always been true to him and that he was my first and only sexual encounter. He's a wonderful person, Bob. I've already told you that. He's done everything he could for Ray and our two other children and been the best husband and father in the world. In my own way I love him very much and I won't hurt him. I won't disillusion him. I can't … I just can't. If you only knew what he thinks of me, how much he loves me and looks up to me, you might understand. He fell madly in love with me at first sight. I'm an idol in his mind, high on a pedestal where I can do no wrong nor could I ever have done wrong. There is nothing he won't do for me. No, Bob, I won't bring George into this. I refuse to."

The well became a pool and spilled over, running slowly down her cheeks. She dabbed at the tears with her handkerchief and then covered her mouth and cheek with one hand in despair. "I'm sorry," she said. "I didn't mean to make a scene."

Bob could say nothing. He could not even imagine a husband and wife having such deep feelings for each other. He was sincerely touched. He patted her free hand in sympathy and remained quiet, waiting for her to speak again.

In a short time she had regained her composure. She looked at Bob and blurted out her idea. "There's only one thing that I can think of to do," she said.

"What is it?" he asked. "I can't think of anything. It would be wonderful if you have an idea."

"Blood tests," she said.

"Blood tests?" he seemed surprised. "Do you mean to determine whether or not I am Ray's father?"

"What else can we do?" she asked in answer to his question. "At least we will know once and for all."

"No, that's out of the question completely." He ground out his cigarette, breaking it into two pieces as he did so.

"Why? Why is it out of the question?" she asked.

"I can think of at least three reasons offhand. The first is that there would be a scandal. The second is that the tests might prove that I definitely am the father. What would that do to George? Third, if the tests show that I might be or that I definitely am Ray's father, then we're back to where we started with the same problem. And we have to assume that it is possible to keep the goings-on a secret from Lorene and Ray and George," he said before adding, "which it isn't. The only positive outcome would be if the tests prove that I am not the father. But it's too big a risk to take."

Allison still felt that it could be worked out satisfactorily. "If the tests show that you could not have been the father, then, as you stated, there is no problem," she said. "If it shows that you are the father, then we will have to deal with it at that time. We may have to tell the children." She had given the entire idea a great deal of thought, and she was determined not to disregard it in such haste.

"Neither Lorene nor Ray, or even George, would have to know why the tests are being done. We will tell them that it is advisable for them to get complete medical checkups if they intend to get married," she argued. "A blood test is routine in a checkup and is required in New York when you get a marriage license. Therefore, they will not suspect anything. I can suggest to George that he go for a checkup too, when Ray goes. He hasn't had one in years, and he really should go anyway. No one would have to know that you were having blood tests also. As for the results, well, if it is proven that George is really Ray's father," she hesitated here for a moment, "that is, if the possibility of your being the parent is eliminated, then we have solved our problem. If you are not eliminated, then, granted, we are back where we started but," and she quoted the old axiom, "nothing ventured, nothing gained."

Bob was shaking his head no as she spoke, so she continued without waiting for a reply.

"There wouldn't be any scandal because no one except the doctors would know what was going on. Can't you see, Bob, that it's the only way? We have to find out."

"No, I can't see," he answered. "Do you think that the ordinary lab technician could perform such a test? I doubt it. This is work for a specialist. It would be impossible to hide the truth. Ignoring for a moment the implications for our families, just think of the publicity, of the scandal. The papers will turn this into a dirty, sordid story of illicit love. None of us will be able to walk the street with our heads up. I'm a respected man in my community, an important man in the business world. I can't afford to let myself get mixed up in a mess like that. No, Allison, I won't do it. I won't."

"I can't believe what I'm hearing, Bob. What makes you think the newspaper will even care about this story, even if they were able to find out? You seem more concerned about yourself than solving the problem. At least let's talk to the doctor first and find out what has to be done. Let's find out exactly what is involved. I still think that we can eliminate any scandal." Allison was adamant.

"No, I won't have any part of it. But I just had another thought. I know what my blood type is and also Lorene's. I imagine you know George's because he was in the service and we all knew our blood type. Do you know Ray's? If Ray doesn't have a blood type that could have come from me, then George is his father and there is no problem." Bob was relieved. He thought he had the answer. "Do you know their blood types?"

"Of course. They are both A positive."

Bob's face fell. "No help there," he said, disappointed. "So am I."

"I don't think it's really the scandal that is bothering you," she said. "I think that you're afraid. You're afraid that you might find out that you *are* the father of my son. All these years you haven't admitted it to yourself. You could always say, 'I may not be; it may be George.' But now that the chips are down, I don't think you want to know. You're afraid to know. You're afraid to accept the responsibility or admit that you may have an illegitimate son." She had become quite vehement, and her words were sharp and cutting. "You are so self-serving. How do you think I feel knowing that my son may be the result of my first and only true love and not of my husband? Yes, Bob, you were the love of my life, and I thought it was reciprocal. Do you think this is easy for me? Stop thinking only of yourself."

"You're being cruel, Allison, and only because you're hurt. Our past sins are being thrown in our faces, and you don't know how to hide them. Neither do I."

"They weren't sins," she said. "We were in love, and I thought we were getting married."

They both sat silently after that, neither knowing exactly what to say.

"But I'll find a way. I have to," he finally said.

"George mustn't know," she repeated. "He must not find out."

"I thought we might work something out," Bob said. "I thought we would because our interests are in common. But I see that I was wrong."

"What do you mean? I'm fully cooperative and came up with a partial solution. It's you who is the stubborn one. Life has certainly changed you, Bob."

"Your main and only concern is for George," Bob replied. "I may be cruel when I say this, but at least I'm being truthful. I don't give a damn about George. I only care about Lorene. I don't want to see her hurt or blunder into an unfortunate marriage because of me."

"Would you deliberately ruin my marriage to spare your daughter?" she asked. "And do you think I want to see my son in an unfortunate marriage?"

"Would you deliberately ruin my daughter to spare your husband?" he asked in return.

Neither had a reply; neither could have one. Each one was so self-involved that neither had any sincere understanding of the other side.

"I think I'd better go now," Allison said presently.

"I guess there's nothing more we can do together," he said.

"Nothing," she replied. "Bob," she added as she rose to leave, "I was really in love with you back then, and seeing you now has stirred up those old feelings. I guess I will always love you. I would have divorced George if you had said you wanted me. You broke my heart. I never understood why you wouldn't marry me. We were so much in love. I really don't know who fathered Ray, but I do know that George is truly his father. Nothing can change that, not even blood tests. But do you realize that we never talked about Ray? How will all this affect him? How will he react if he should find out that George is not his father? How will he feel if he has to give up the love of his life? You're only concerned with how this affects you. You haven't even mentioned how this has truly affected your wife. Do you think she heard all this and just accepted it? If you told her the truth, then she knows that I was the love of your life. How do you think she feels? Don't you think she's hurt? You are completely insensitive and self-serving and a big disappointment." With those closing remarks, she started for the door.

Bob remained seated.. There were no goodbyes. He stood up as he watched her disappear from sight and bemoaned the unfortunate turn of events that had taken place.

"Another martini," he ordered as he sat down again. One more was just what he needed.

Chapter 18

Gloria was waiting for Bob, as usual, that night when the 5:35 train pulled into the Woodmere station. She watched him alight from the smoking car and head slowly in her direction.

"Well?" she asked anxiously through the open window before he even had a chance to get into the car. "What happened?"

"Nothing," he replied. "Absolutely nothing." His walk and look were of an older man; his shoulders were hunched, and his steps were dragging and slow.

"What do you mean?" she asked as he slid into the seat beside her. "I've been calling you at your office all afternoon, but you weren't in."

"I know. I had some thinking to do, and I spent the entire afternoon doing it."

"Didn't you meet Allison?"

During this time of questioning, they had been sitting in the car making no attempt at starting for home, and had the drivers of the cars behind them not become impatient with the wait, they would have remained longer. But, as fate would have it, the insistent honking of horns brought them back to the realization that this was not the place to talk. Gloria turned the key and accelerated the car.

"But did you see her?" she asked again after a few moments of silence.

"Yes," he answered briefly.

"Well?" she asked. "What did she say? Don't make me pull it out of you."

"It was no good," he answered. "She wants us to have blood tests to try to prove Ray's paternity."

"That would be of no help unless you were eliminated," she said. "But actually it's not a bad idea."

"It's a terrible idea. I disagreed because, as you said, it would be of no help unless I was eliminated. But she stuck to her guns: she wants blood tests."

"What are you going to do?" Her eyes were intent on the road, but her ears and mind were concentrating on his words.

The traffic light on the corner they were approaching turned to yellow, and Gloria braked the car slowly.

"I'm not sure yet, not yet," he replied thoughtfully.

They sat silently through the red light and for the remainder of the drive. The decision was an important and difficult one. When they parked in their driveway, Bob exited quickly and walked rapidly to the house. Gloria followed, her high heels clicking behind him.

Inside, the dining room table was set for supper, and the aroma of pot roast and potato pancakes filled the entire downstairs area. Lorene had heard the car come to a halt in the driveway and was coming slowly down the stairs from her bedroom as her father entered the house. Their glances met for an instant before Lorene turned away. Bob could see questions, doubt, and insecurity in Lorene's eyes. He felt great pangs of guilt. Here was the one person in the world he had never wanted to hurt, the one he protected from cuts and bruises as a child, from disillusionment and heartaches as an adolescent. This was the girl he vowed he would go to the ends of the earth to please and to make happy. And now that she was an adult, he was wrecking every image and dream of himself that he had worked so hard to build up in her. Every semblance of love and respect that she had ever had he was tearing to shreds. He saw the bewilderment and the hate that was building up. It was all there in her eyes. How he yearned to reach out, to cradle her in his arms, and to tell her everything was all right, that he loved her deeply.

I can't let this continue much longer, he thought. *I must decide and act quickly before I drive my daughter from me completely.*

"Good evening, Dad," Lorene said, walking past him into the dining room. The usual welcoming kiss was not offered. "Dinner smells great, Mom. Is it ready?" she asked.

"In a minute," Gloria answered. She turned to Bob and said, "You'd better get washed up now, dear." She was trying hard to act naturally so Lorene would not suspect that she was upset with Bob.

"Yes, I'm going," he answered.

"Dad?"

He stopped suddenly, his hand on the banister, one foot on the first riser.

"Yes, Lorene?"

"Are you going to see Ray tonight?"

"No, honey, I'm not." He said it quietly and in a matter-of-fact manner.

"I kind of thought so. I made an excuse for you. I told Ray that you had to go out early."

"Why did you do that?" he asked. "Why didn't you just tell him that I'm opposed to your engagement? That would be the truth."

Tears came to her eyes with her answer. "You didn't expect me to tell him that you were a mean, stubborn, unreasonable man, did you? That would be the truth too."

"You're not being fair, Lorene," he replied as he stepped backward into the foyer and turned to face her.

"Are you being fair, Dad?"

"Would you rather have me see him and tell him, to his face, that I am absolutely opposed?"

"There's no reason why you shouldn't bless us." She turned her back to him and, with her eyes on the floor, walked back into the dining room, where she slumped into a corner chair.

"Look at me, Lorene," Bob pleaded. "Look at me."

She looked up slowly. "What?" she asked.

"I had an excellent idea this afternoon. Now I realize that you may be in no mood for an idea like this at the moment, but I want you to think it over and give it your true consideration."

"What is it?" she asked suspiciously.

"Ray has one more year of school, doesn't he?"

"Yes."

"How would you like to study in Europe this coming year?"

"Dad!" she snapped back, annoyed.

"Now wait a minute. You're both young and should have a chance to test your love. Being in Europe for a year will be a wonderful opportunity for you, and you'll be that much more certain when you return. And so will he. You could spend the year in France, or Switzerland, or any country you would like. There are good schools in Europe. Any girl would jump at the chance."

"In other words, you want to send me away where Ray and I can't see each other. You hope that a year apart will break us up," she replied bitterly.

"I didn't say that."

"No, but you might just as well for that's what you meant."

"You've nothing to lose," Bob replied, "and," he continued, hating himself for the lies he was contriving, "everything to gain."

"I won't go," Lorene answered quickly.

"Why not?"

"I want to be able to see Ray, not be separated from him. I know, and Ray knows, that this is the real thing. I think that you know it too. We don't have to be oceans apart to prove it to anyone. One year's engagement is enough proof."

"But Lorene—"

"No, Dad," she interrupted. "I won't go. And furthermore," she paused briefly, wetting her lips with her tongue a few times before she continued, "I didn't want to say what I'm going to now. I hoped I wouldn't have to, but I have no choice. We will be engaged, and married, whether you like it or not—whether it is with your permission or not."

"You really don't mean it." Her words had come as a sudden blow.

"We're both over age. I don't need your permission to be married. If you persist in your idiotic objections, we'll go ahead anyway, without your consent or your blessings. We don't want it that way, but if it has to be, then that's the way it will be."

"You wouldn't, Lorene. You wouldn't," he pleaded.

"Yes, Dad, I would and I will."

"You can't really mean it," he said. "You're bluffing. Would you so completely disobey your mother and me? Would you take such a step knowing how we feel?"

"Yes, I would if you gave me no other choice." Her answer was simple and direct.

At that moment Gloria entered from the kitchen. She was busily drying her hands on a linen dish towel and wearing a large flowered apron over her dress.

"Dinner is ready," she announced.

"I'm not very hungry," Bob answered as he started up the stairs. "I think I'll skip supper tonight."

"What is it?" Gloria asked. "What's the matter? What happened between you two while I was in the kitchen?" She asked the questions but knew what the answers would be.

"Your daughter has made her intentions clear," he said, looking over the railing. "She's going to marry Ray no matter what we say. Unfortunately, she's eighteen years old and can do as she pleases. I offered her a year of study in Europe to test their love. She turned me down."

Gloria stood quietly and watched him disappear into the upstairs hall. Then she turned to Lorene and asked, "Is that what you told him?"

"Yes."

"Why would you threaten your dad like that?"

"I didn't think you'd ever ask a question like that, Mom. I thought you knew and that you would understand."

"I guess I do know," Gloria answered. "And I understand also. You see, honey, I understand you, but I understand your father too."

"What is there to understand about Dad's point of view?"

"Quite a bit."

"Oh, sure. I'm too young. We haven't known each other long enough. Ray's future is too insecure, et cetera, et cetera, et cetera," she said in disgust, mimicking Bob as she did so. "I won't even argue those points with you. I'm too tired to disagree anymore anyway."

"Lorene—"

"Please, Mother, no more. We're going to be married just as soon as Ray is graduated. Now, can we eat?"

"Yes, I suppose so," Gloria answered. "But there is one more thing I want to say."

"What?"

"I think you should think carefully about the offer your dad made. It's not a bad idea. And a year is really not that long. It's really only nine months, September to May. In fact, it doesn't have to be a year. What if you went to Europe for one semester? It would test your love and appease your father. Maybe you should discuss it with Ray. I'm sure he would not want you to miss out on a chance like this."

"Mom, I know you're trying to mediate this situation. I appreciate that. But I am standing firm. I don't want to go anywhere."

"But he's in Troy, New York. You won't see each other anyway. We will never agree to your going up there and staying in a hotel. And from what you tell me, Ray needs his weekends to study so he can't come here."

"I don't know what we'll do, but we'll find a way. There are always Thanksgiving and Christmas and long holiday weekends. And we can talk on the phone. If I were in Europe, the cost of the calls would be phenomenal. Now, Mom, please, drop it. Let's eat."

"Okay, dig in." She passed the pot roast casserole dish to Lorene. "Help yourself." To herself she acknowledged that there really was nothing more to say.

Chapter 19

After dinner both Gloria and Lorene went to their respective bedrooms on the second floor, which had three bedrooms. The other was a guest room, usually used by Bob's parents who had taken an early retirement to Florida or Gloria's parents who lived in Chicago. It was simply furnished with a queen-size bed, a chest of drawers, and a TV set. The second bedroom was Lorene's. It was furnished in a very feminine manner with a gilt-framed mirror above a French Provincial dresser. There was a skirted dressing table, a nightstand alongside a single bed, a French Provincial desk, and a TV. The master bedroom contained all Danish furniture. In addition to a king-sized bed, it held a triple dresser for Gloria with a framed mirror above it, a chest of drawers for Bob, two nightstands, and a television set on a small bookcase. Venetian blinds covered the windows. All the rooms were tastefully done and reflected Gloria's decorating ability.

The door to the master bedroom was closed when Gloria reached the room. She opened the door to find the room in darkness.

"Bob," she called out softly from the entrance.

"I'm here, on the bed," he replied.

"What have you been doing?"

"Thinking. Just thinking."

She walked over to the bed and, sitting down beside him, ran her fingers slowly through his hair and over his brow.

"What should I do, Gloria? What should I do?" he pleaded.

"It doesn't seem that there are many options," she answered as she continued to stroke his brow. As much as she disagreed with him, she still felt sorry for the anguish he was going through.

"Allison has one," he replied softly. "But I can't see that as the answer. I want to protect Lorene, and if the test results showed my paternity, that would not protect her."

"Yes, that was one solution, and the other was to tell Lorene and hope she understands and forgives you—which she might," Gloria added.

"No, absolutely no!" he said very emphatically. "And if I tell her, look at the position I would put her in. What would she tell Ray? Would she tell him the truth? Would they decide to take the risk and get married anyway? No, no, I can't tell her."

Bob sat up straight. Clenching his right fist, he rolled it slowly but roughly in the palm of his other hand. "How can I deliberately drive her from me, make her hate me for my actions as a young soldier and my actions as her father? She will curse me for ruining her life. She'd never forgive me for the loss of the love of her life."

"You're making her hate you now, Bob," Gloria replied. "And look at the position you are putting *me* in. You're making me jeopardize my relationship with her too. And this isn't helping our own relationship."

"I know. I saw it in her eyes tonight." Bob ignored Gloria's concern about her relationship with Lorene or with him. He was thinking only of his daughter's feelings for him. "But this is different. She hates me now for hurting her. That will disappear as soon as the next young man comes along, and he will, and she'll fall in love again. But if I tell her what I've done, she'll hate me for the deception I've lived and played. Don't all parents have something in their past that they don't want their children to know? Is it a crime to keep it a secret? They are young and don't see us as emotional beings with sexual desires and faults as well as virtues. They put us up on a pedestal. Our pasts, our youth are only fairy tales to our children. Can a child picture a parent as an infant, a toddler? Can a daughter picture her father as a man, in bed with her mother conceiving her or just making love? If I bring her world crashing down around her, I will have lost everything I've worked so hard to achieve all these years—her respect and her love. She'll never get over it and never forgive me. I'll become the man of evil who in his mischievous past wrecked her life. Ray will forever be the boy she loved but couldn't have—a *Romeo and Juliet* story.

"Perhaps you're right," Gloria said. "If you are, then there is no answer, for you've rejected the only two possibilities."

"Gloria, I don't understand it. Why can't children be like they were years ago? We listened to our parents. When they said no, we obeyed. When my parents told me that I had to marry a Jewish girl, that they would accept nothing less, I listened to them. When—"

"One minute," Gloria blurted out. "Repeat what you just said."

"I said I obeyed my parents and did what they said."

"Not that part. The part about who you could marry."

"My parents told me that I had to marry a Jewish girl. My mother was quite religious, so it was important to her."

"Do you hear yourself? Do you realize what you said?" Gloria was amazed at this new revelation.

"What do you mean?" Bob asked. "I don't understand."

"Bob, you knew the whole time you were seeing Allison that you would never marry her because she wasn't Jewish. You knew she loved you and held out hopes that you would marry her. But you used other excuses, like you weren't ready, you were too young, the war, et cetera. You never told her the truth. The truth would have made it so much easier for her. Most likely she would not have pursued you the way she did. I can't believe you were such a heel! Did you care for her at all?" Gloria wanted to hear what he had to say.

"I was very fond of her."

"Don't hedge. Be honest. If she had been Jewish, would you have married her?"

"Yes." He said it so quietly that she almost didn't hear the answer.

"So you did love her." It was a statement, but Gloria meant it as a question.

"Yes."

Pools of tears filled Gloria's eyes. She was so hurt. He had lied to her about his true feelings for Allison and why he hadn't married her. Gloria felt like she was a runner-up. "You are unbelievable," she said in anger. "You were completely self-serving, you were inconsiderate, and your behavior was despicable. You thought only of yourself and how your parents would react. You gave no thought to the poor girl whom you might have impregnated. What is wrong with you? You couldn't tell the truth then, and you can't now. I always thought you were a man of honor. I thought you were someone I could trust and rely on. Obviously, I was wrong. You haven't changed. But I have. My feelings for you have truly changed now that I know what you are really like. Did you love me when you married me, or was I just the Jewish girl your parents wanted? I don't know what to think anymore." Gloria burst into tears. Her life was falling apart.

"Don't be so dramatic," he answered unsympathetically. "I loved Allison then, but that was years ago. When I met you, I fell in love with you. Your attacks on me are unfair and unjust. I've been a good husband, and I've tried to consider you always and do everything I could for you. We've always worked together, and I need you now more than ever."

"No, Bob. No. I'm not with you. You created this mess, and you have to get out of it." Gloria was determined.

"But there *is* an answer. That's what I was thinking about. There is a way out." Bob seemed hopeful.

"I don't believe it. What horrible plan do you have now? Who are you going to hurt this time?" Gloria was cynical.

"There's one person who might understand."

"Who?" she asked.

"Ray."

"Ray?" She couldn't believe what she heard. "Ray? You don't mean you would tell Ray, do you?" She was incredulous.

"That's just what I mean." He got up from the bed and, while pacing the floor, told her of his plan.

"I'll meet Ray privately somewhere and tell him the whole story. He's a man, virile and young; he must have had girls and lots of them. He's the only one who could understand what happened twenty-four years ago and why. He'll realize that he can't marry Lorene, and he'll break it up on some pretense or other."

"That's cruel, Bob. You're going to tell him that his mother was fooling around with you while she was married? If it was before she was married, that would be different. But it's not right to dump this all on him. And what if he doesn't understand?"

"Then he'll hate me. So what? I don't care who hates me as long as it's not Lorene."

"You don't care if I hate you? You're disillusioning me more and more. Now, here's something you have to consider: what if he tells Lorene?" she asked.

"He won't, not if he loves her. He won't want to hurt her, and he certainly won't want his parents to know that he knows."

"You're giving him credit for a lot more character than you had, Bob. Assuming he won't tell Lorene. How can you do this to him? It's cruel."

"Cruel? How is it cruel?" he asked.

"If you can't see it, then you really don't have an ounce of feeling or understanding. Ray has been raised believing George to be his father. How can you tell him now that his family may not be the family he thinks it is? It may ruin his life and the marriage of his parents. It may affect his relationship with his mother and his father. Don't chance ruining this young man's life. And don't forget that you would be breaking up his relationship with Lorene. It would mean he will be losing the love of his life."

"He won't tell his parents. There would be no need to. What I tell him he'll keep to himself. And what if he is shocked and heartbroken? So what?"

Gloria couldn't believe what she was hearing. "You really don't care about what you may do to him, do you?"

"No, I don't care. Why should I? All I want is my daughter's happiness. I'll do anything, anything to get it for her and to protect her at the same time."

"You are a self-centered bastard," she said bitterly. "I think you are really trying to protect yourself. You can't accept responsibility. If you could, you would have a blood test, which Allison agreed to. She's willing to risk the results, and so should you. But you're too much of a narcissist; you only care about yourself. You don't care about me, either. You don't give a damn about how all of this is affecting me."

"Yes, you are right. I'm protecting myself and Lorene. That's all I care about."

"No. You are only protecting yourself. Can't you think of the consequences to this boy? If I were his mother, I would never want him to know unless it was absolutely necessary. Why should he know that his paternity is uncertain? Why should he learn of his mother's indiscretions as a young girl? Only if the blood tests showed that you were his father would he have to know. By that time, you may think of another way to handle things."

"Do you want Lorene to know?" he asked.

"No, I don't want that either. But if it is necessary then she will have to know. But we won't know if it's necessary until you do blood tests. Just think, Bob, if George is really Ray's father, the children can go on with their love affair and get married in June. It could be a happy ending."

He reached out for her and took her hands in his. "There's no other way, Gloria. I don't agree with your reasoning. One of the two of them has to be told. Who shall we make miserable—our child or a stranger's?"

"And don't you think Lorene will be miserable if Ray breaks up with her? She'll spend her life wondering just as Allison did, I'm sure. In your mind there are no choices. Telling Ray is the only solution."

"There isn't any other way."

`"But it's so cruel. I keep saying it, but it's true. This is a cruel thing to do."

"The hell with cruelty," Bob answered sharply. "I'd give my life for my daughter, and if necessary I'll give someone else's."

Gloria began to sob. She couldn't believe what was happening. Bob was not very sympathetic. "It will be okay," he said. "Just wait and see."

"When do you plan to see Ray?" she asked, trying vainly to dry her tears.

"Tomorrow, if I can. I'll call him at his house and make an appointment. I'll pretend, if Allison answers the telephone, that I'm a friend of his."

"More lies. Lies! Lies! Lies!" Her voice rose with each exclamation. "Please reconsider having the blood tests."

"No, *no, no!*" He was emphatic. "Lorene must not know. She mustn't have any idea."

"You don't think I would tell her, do you? But your plan is bad. Don't do this. Please, Bob," she pleaded.

"It will be okay." He tried to reassure her. "In two days this will all be over."

"Not for me. I can never forgive you. I still wish there was some other way that you would accept"

"Well, there isn't. I've thought about it continuously. There's no other way out."

"I can't bear to be in this room with you," Gloria said. "I think you should use the guest room tonight."

`Bob knew when he should argue and when he shouldn't. "Okay," he said. "But believe me, this will all work out." He did not try to appease Gloria.

Chapter 20

Some places have their own peculiar odors likened to them alone that is as much a part of their existence as the structure that houses them. The smell of a new car, a doctor's office, the interior of a delicatessen or florist, the walls of a new home, and thousands of other places are distinguishable by their smells. To Gladys, the most potent of smells was that of gasoline. She remembered vividly that when she was a child and had whooping cough, her mother took her to a gasoline station every day to breathe in the fumes, which were supposed to be a cure for the disease. One of the most impressive odors, however, is the distinctly different hygienic fragrance of the hospital. It surrounds one suddenly upon entrance into the building and immediately filters itself into the body, seemingly driving away all regular oxygen.

Gladys and Ed were both acutely aware of the smell, and she shivered slightly as she inhaled the full extent of the scent into the depths of her lungs. She had never liked hospitals and the aromas had never been pleasant for her, but now they were suddenly obnoxious. She held tightly onto Ed's left hand with her right, and together they walked into the elevator. She barely noticed the sensation of losing her stomach as the elevator moved rapidly upward. They waited nervously, and then the door opened as they reached the third floor. Upon exiting, they turned quickly to their right and found number 310 to be the third room down the hall. The door stood ajar, as most did during visiting hours, revealing a room approximately ten feet by ten feet in size containing a metal hospital bed, one armchair, a straight-backed chair, and a dresser. In one corner, next to the closet door, a sink was attached to the wall underneath a small chromium-framed mirror.

Eileen lay almost prone, the bed tilted upward slightly under her head so that she could assume a more comfortable, almost-sitting position.

"Hi, Mom, Dad," she said, trying to sound cheerful as they entered. Peter stood alongside her, his eyes deep with worry and his mouth set in a grim line.

"How do you feel, darling?" Gladys asked as she leaned forward to kiss her daughter gently on the forehead. She noted that Eileen was extremely pale and especially worn and tired looking.

"Pretty good. I really can't complain." She then added, "Considering what I've gone through. I feel worse about losing the baby."

"Was it very bad, honey?" Ed asked.

"Not too bad. I have some discomfort now, but that's natural they tell me."

"Do they know why it happened?" Gladys asked.

"I had an ovarian cyst. The doctor thinks that is what caused it."

"You never told me about that," Gladys said, feeling a bit hurt. "You never told me you had a cyst." Gladys had never quite cut the apron strings. She had not fully accepted that her daughter was no longer a child whose every ache, trouble, and worry she could share. She did realize that she could no longer be an intimate part of her children's lives when her son, her only other child, had married six months earlier, had moved to his wife's hometown in another state, and was in touch infrequently.

"We didn't want to worry you, Mom."

"You never have to worry about that. I'm your mother. I want to know everything." Then she added, "You look so tired, darling." Actually, she was thinking again how very bad her daughter appeared.

"I guess I am a bit tired. The operation was only this morning, you know," Eileen replied.

"Operation? What do you mean?" Gladys was obviously quite surprised. "You only had a miscarriage, didn't you? That only requires a slight cleaning, a D and C. Why did you have an operation?"

Eileen turned toward Pete and asked, "Didn't you tell them?"

"No," he replied. "I didn't want to on the phone, and I haven't had a chance to see your folks until now."

"Oh," she said simply. "I'm sorry. I wish you had."

"What is this all about?" Gladys asked impatiently.

"Sit down, Mom," Peter said. He pulled the armchair over and placed it directly behind her. She sat down, grasping the two arms as she did so.

"I don't like this," she said. "You're making me very nervous. Something must be wrong, terribly wrong. What is it?" Turning to Ed, she said, "Ed, hold me. I'm frightened about what I'm going to hear."

Ed walked over and put his hands on her shoulders. "It will be all right, honey. Whatever it is, it will be all right," he said. "Eileen is well, and healthy and that's what counts."

"Mom," Eileen began, "it seems that I had more than just the one growth."

"What do you mean? Couldn't they take them out?" Gladys asked.

"Yes, only that … well," Eileen looked to Peter for support and then continued. "They all had to be removed, and they were, surgically."

Gladys sighed deeply in relief. "What was so bad about that? Of course, losing the baby was bad. But from your attitude I expected something awful had happened. If the growths are removed now, then you won't have any more trouble with your pregnancies or any more worry about the growths themselves." She looked up at Ed and smiled. He in turn patted her shoulder gently.

"That's not all," Peter said.

"You don't mean—" Gladys said in alarm, realizing the innuendos involved in a discussion of growths. "You don't mean they were cancerous?" She almost whispered the last word as if she was terribly afraid to utter it aloud because that might mean it was true.

"Oh, no," Eileen added quickly. "Definitely not."

Gladys's mind was set at ease, and she relaxed once again. "Then there's nothing to worry about. You'll recover from this operation, rest up for about six months or maybe more, and you'll be able to start planning for a family again."

"No, Mother," Eileen said. "There won't be any babies, ever."

"What? What are you saying? They're not telling me the truth, are they, Ed? They don't mean it. Eileen, you don't mean it. You mean there won't be babies for a while …"

She looked up at Ed, pleading for reassurance. Becoming a grandmother was such an important part of her dreams that she couldn't imagine it never happening. She didn't even consider her son because she couldn't share in his life. But her daughter lived nearby, and a child could be an integral part of her life. She turned back to Eileen. "Lots of girls have trouble with their first and even second pregnancies. But that doesn't mean that they can't or shouldn't have any more." She was going to fight the truth no matter what.

"You don't understand, Mom. I had a hysterectomy this morning."

Gladys couldn't say anything. She could hardly believe what she had heard. The impact of Eileen's words jolted her back to reality. Finally, her eyes filled with tears, and she said, "But you are so young." She repeated softly, "So young. I'm so sorry, so very sorry." She brought her hands up to cover her eyes, and she sobbed gently into them.

"It had to be done," Peter interjected.

"I'm sure," Ed contributed. "The doctor would not have done it if it wasn't imperative."

"What will you do?" Gladys asked of Eileen when she had regained her composure.

"Mom, we won't remain childless. We will look at all the options and make a decision. There is a good chance we will adopt. We feel that if we raise a child, it will be as much ours as if I had borne it. Peter and I began considering this after I lost the first baby."

Gladys shook her head. "That isn't always so easy to do. So many people want babies, and there are so few available."

"Don't be a wet blanket, Mom," Eileen said. "Don't be pessimistic. We know what the problems are. But we want a child— that's all we care about. If we can't do it legally, we'll go to the gray market and if necessary overseas. We don't care about the color or the nationality. But we will get a child, somewhere, somehow." Eileen was emphatic.

Gladys nodded slowly. She still couldn't believe it.

"I'm sorry," the nurse interrupted from the open doorway, "but visiting hours are over. You'll have to leave now."

"We'll see you tomorrow, honey," Ed said. "I'll take Mother home now. Are you coming, Peter?"

"In a minute. You start down, and I'll catch up with you."

Ed nodded, and as he and Gladys headed for the door, he compassionately called back over his shoulder. "Try to get a good night's rest, honey. You'll feel better in the morning."

"I will, Dad. Good night."

Ed led Gladys down the hall, into the elevator, through the lobby, and out into the street. She hadn't spoken since her departure from the room, but now, as she breathed in the cool fresh air of the evening, she sighed gently. "That smells so good." Then she added, "I don't understand how Eileen could be so good after just having surgery. She didn't seem to have much pain at all."

"Honey, did you see the IV? They are pumping her with painkillers. She'll begin to feel it more tomorrow."

"I guess you're right. It's not like years ago when you suffered for days."

"Let's go home," Ed suggested as he steered her to the street and to their parked car.

"Yes, Gladys answered. "I want to go home."

Chapter 21

It was a beautiful summer morning. The sun was shining brightly, and the humidity was low. Bob was up and dressed early, anxiously anticipating his meeting with Ray. But first he had to call him and make an appointment.

What if he doesn't want to meet with me? he thought. Then he shrugged off the idea. *Of course he'll want to meet with me. He's been asking for a meeting.*

Now that the final moment of action had arrived, Bob began to lose his courage. He was afraid that Allison might answer the phone. What would he say to her? Or what if George answered? How would he explain himself? He had thought he could pretend to be one of Ray's friends, but he realized that if someone asked questions, it would be awkward.

No, he thought. *If Allison or George answers, I'll just say I want to talk to Ray. I'll simply say that Ray requested a meeting with me and that I'd like to make an appointment with him. Honesty is the best policy,* he concluded.

There was a phone in the master bedroom, but Gloria was getting dressed there and he preferred to make his call privately. The other phone was on the wall in the kitchen, so Bob decided to use that one. Once in the kitchen he began to get cold feet. The whole situation was unpleasant. He sat down on a kitchen chair and lit a cigarette.

"This is silly," he said, bolstering himself. "There is nothing to be nervous about."

Bob had the phone number; he had gotten it when he called Allison. He took the receiver off the hook, looked at the sheet of paper that bore the number, and dialed it carefully. He could hear the phone ringing. One ... two ... three ... and then there was an answer.

"Hello?" It was Ray. Bob was relieved.

"Hello, Ray. This is Mr. Ruthers. Did I get you at a bad time?"

"No, sir, not at all. What can I do for you?" Ray was obviously quite surprised to hear from Bob.

"Well, Lorene told me that you would like to meet with me." Bob thought, *That's good. I've turned this around so the meeting is his idea.*

"Well," Ray answered, "I would. Can I come over this evening?"

"That's not what I had in mind. I thought we could meet for lunch today. How does that sound?"

Ray was nonplussed. He didn't understand what was going on. First, Mr. Ruthers had absolutely refused to meet with him, and now he wanted to meet for lunch. It didn't make sense to Ray.

"I suppose that's okay," he replied. "But you'll be at work, and I really don't want to come into the city."

"Oh, no. I'm not going to work today. We can meet on the island."

"Okay, where and when?" Now Ray was truly confused. Not only did Mr. Ruthers want to meet with him at lunchtime, but he was also giving up going to work.

"There's a nice diner in Far Rockaway. It's on Far Rockaway Boulevard, at the corner of Forty-Third Street. It's called Starlight."

"Let me write that down. Far Rockaway Boulevard and Forty-Third Street? And it's called Starlight. Is that right?"

"You got it. Is twelve thirty okay?"

"Sure."

"There's one other thing," Bob added. "Don't tell anyone that you and I are meeting."

"What? Why the secret? What's going on? I don't like to keep secrets from my parents. And what about Lorene? Does she know we are meeting? Will she be there?" Ray was loaded with questions because the situation was so peculiar.

"I can't explain now," Bob answered. "I'll tell you everything when I meet you for lunch. Will you be there?"

"Of course, sir, if you want me to be." Ray was anxious to please his future father-in-law, and he was willing to agree to anything the man proposed.

"Good. I'll see you then." Bob hung up, greatly relieved that the first step had been taken but apprehensive about what was to come.

Ray put the receiver back in the cradle. He was shocked and completely confused. *Why did Mr. Ruthers call me to meet for lunch? Why did he choose a restaurant in another town? How come he is taking the day off of work? Why should I not tell anyone that we're meeting? Well*, he thought, *I'll know soon enough.*

Bob had researched the restaurants in Far Rockaway the evening before. He carefully selected the Starlight diner in Far Rockaway because of its distance from his natural habitat and the fact that no one would know him there. He and Ray could talk undisturbed.

When Gloria came downstairs for breakfast, she was prepared to drive Bob to the station to get his train into the city.

"I guess you're going in late today. It's way past your regular time," she said. "You didn't ask me to drive you to the station."

"I'm not going to work. I'm meeting Ray."

"Did you speak with him already? You called him so early?" she asked.

"I wasn't even aware of the time. But it wasn't too early for him."

"Is he meeting you?"

"Yes, at twelve thirty."

"Are you sure you want to do this?" Gloria asked as she poured herself a cup of coffee.

"Yes, there is no other way."

"You know I am opposed. Does that matter to you at all?"

"I wish you could see it my way. I'm sorry you don't agree, but it has to be this way."

"Then there is nothing more to say," Gloria said as she picked up her coffee and headed out of the kitchen.

"Where are you going?" Bob called out after her.

"Anywhere I can be alone. And keep your voice down so you don't wake Lorene."

Left alone, Bob decided to leave. He walked to the front door and quietly closed it behind him. He didn't know where he was going, and he didn't care. He just wanted to get into his car and drive. He just wanted the hours to pass until it was time to meet Ray. He stopped at a gas station to fill up. He spotted a House of Waffles restaurant and decided that he would like a good waffle, so he went in and spent an hour dawdling over waffles and coffee in a place he normally would never have inhabited. It seemed fairly clean, but the booths were old, the red leatherette seats were torn in a few places, and the mica tabletops were chipped. The waffles, however, were delicious. After an hour he realized he shouldn't sit there any longer, so he paid the bill and left. He still had about an hour and a half to kill, and even a slow ride to Far Rockaway would not take that much time. Then he thought, *I can walk on the boardwalk. Far Rockaway has a lovely boardwalk, and I haven't been there in years.* With a definite direction in mind, Bob pressed on the gas pedal to speed up the car. It took just less than a half hour to get to the beach and park the car. He still had an hour to go. He walked up the street, which was lined with bungalows. He didn't know which street it was, and it didn't matter since they all led to the beach and the boardwalk. Each street was a twin of the next. One bungalow stood alongside another, occupied only in the summer by city dwellers attempting to escape the summer's heat. The rich urban inhabitants went to the Catskill Mountains for the summer, either to a hotel or to a bungalow colony. There was sand on top of the concrete sidewalks, brought there by people leaving the beach. When he reached the boardwalk, he took a deep breath. The salty air was refreshing. He sat on a wooden bench facing the beach and watched the children playing in the sand, children and adults jumping the waves, and sunbathers stretched out on multicolored blankets. Suddenly he became aware of the time. It was noon. He had wanted to arrive early, a good deal before the appointed time. He was only a few blocks away, and it was time to go.

When he walked into the Starlight diner, he spotted a booth in the rear of the establishment and made his way to it after reading a sign that said, "Seat yourself." Now, sitting in the booth, facing the entrance, he wondered just how he would begin. He hadn't planned this out. He couldn't just say, "My boy, brace yourself for a shock. I may be your father." No, he had to be diplomatic. He had to be tactful.

"Mr. Ruthers?" Ray's voice asked suddenly.

Bob had been so deep in thought that he hadn't seen or heard the boy enter.

"Yes, Ray. Sit down, won't you?"

Ray slid into the booth facing him and raised the subject immediately. "You wanted to see me, Mr. Ruthers. What was it you had on your mind?"

Bob had hoped that he wouldn't force the issue. He felt that he had to get into this slowly in his own way.

"Well, first," he stalled, "I was told *you* wanted to see *me*."

"Yes, but Lorene said you refused to see me. I was going to tell you that Lorene and I want to get married. I wanted your permission to marry your daughter. I'm sure that's not why you wanted to meet with me today. Why are we meeting now?"

"Won't you have a drink first?" Bob asked, again trying to stall things.

"No, thank you, sir." He drew a pack of Chesterfields from his breast pocket and a lighter from his pants pocket. He extracted a cigarette, lit it, and placed the remainder of the pack on the table beside him. He held the lighter in his hand and played idly with it as he watched Bob. He was waiting for Bob to start the conversation.

"I know that you are anxious to find out what this is all about," Bob said, "but you'll have to bear with me. I must tell you this in my own way."

`"Whatever you say, sir," Ray answered politely, though he was a bit weary of the mystery Bob was creating.

"I guess you can say that I want to tell you a story. It has its beginning many years ago during the Second World War. I was stationed down south, in South Carolina, and had just received my first pass. I went to a USO dance, and I met your mother there."

"You knew my mother back then?" Ray was amazed. "I had no idea you knew one another. Does she remember who you are? Have you been in touch?"

"Take it slowly, Ray. Let me tell it my way. We met, we liked each other, and we dated for quite a while. And we had an intimate relationship. Then I was shipped to a base in Texas. We kept up correspondence, but both your mother and I were dating other people. Your father was one of them, and when he proposed to her, she said yes."

Ray was listening intently. This was all news to him, and he was finding it fascinating as well as disturbing. "You and my mother had an intimate relationship? This is hard to believe."

"This was common during the war. The servicemen were away from home and lonely, and lots of romances took place. But let me continue. The day after your mother and father were married," Bob continued, ignoring Ray's remarks, "your father was transferred to a base in Texas. They knew he was being transferred, and that's why they rushed their marriage. His base in Texas was not far from mine. Your mother came out to be with him. They got married and then he was shipped overseas almost immediately."

"My mother told me how she met my dad and how she followed him to Texas," Ray interjected.

"Well, your mother knew that I was also in Texas. So when your father was shipped out, she contacted me and came to visit me. We spent the next week together." Bob was trying to put it as gently as he could. He hoped that Ray would put one and one together on his own.

Ray's facial expression began to change. As the story sank in and he realized just what Bob was telling him, he first expressed shock and then disbelief. "Just one minute," he said indignantly. "I won't have you making up such lies about my mother. How dare you say such things? I can see you'll stoop to any level to keep Lorene and me apart. My mother would never have done what you say."

"We thought we were in love," Bob said, trying to defend himself and Allison.

"Then why did she marry my father? If you were in love, why didn't the two of you get married?"

"I didn't want to," Bob said. "Your mother was willing." After a pause, he added, "I guess she fell in love with your father too."

"My mother told me she became pregnant shortly after getting married. When did my mother become pregnant?" he asked.

"We don't know. It was sometime in that time period."

"Are you saying," Ray began, "that both you and my father had relations with my mother around the same time? Are you saying that you may be my … my …" He couldn't get the word out.

"Your father, Ray. I might be your father."

"I don't believe you. You're a liar. You made up a story to keep Lorene and me apart. I know my mother. She wouldn't do anything like that. She loves my father. She wouldn't cheat on him."

"Unfortunately, it's all quite true. I can prove it, and so can your mother."

"Do you realize what you are saying, Mr. Ruthers?" Ray asked. "You know I would never ask my mother such a thing, so you're gambling that I will just accept your story."

"I know perfectly well what I'm saying. That's why I had to tell you."

Ray shook his head and ran his fingers through his hair nervously." You wouldn't make up a story like this. You couldn't."

At that moment, the waitress appeared with two glasses of water. "What will you gentlemen have?" she asked.

"Nothing for me," Ray answered. "I'm not hungry."

"I'll have a BLT," Bob responded. Then to Ray he said, "Have something, please. We can't just sit here, and you have to eat."

"Okay. I'll have the same thing."

"Thanks," the waitress said as she picked up the menus and scurried off.

"Did you make this up, just to break us up?" Ray asked. "I know you've been opposed to me from the start."

"No, I wouldn't do that, Ray. It's true. God help me, every word is true."

"My mother, a … a …," he started to say, but he couldn't finish his sentence.

"Don't say it, Ray. I never did. Your mother is and was a fine person. We were very fond of each other before she met your father. As I told you, we fancied we were in love."

"My father—does he know? Does he suspect?"

"No, and your mother doesn't want him to."

"You spoke with my mother?" Ray asked. He never suspected that.

"Yes, we met for lunch."

"Does my mother know that you're telling me all this?' Ray asked.

"God, no, and don't ever tell her that I told you. It would break her heart. Don't you see, Ray? I had to tell you. I had no other way of breaking up your engagement to Lorene. You might be related. I hoped that you would understand and forgive what happened so many years ago. You're a man, you've slept with girls, and you know what it's like to—"

Ray interrupted, "To want a lay? Is that what my mother was to you? Is that all she meant to you?"

"Please, Ray, don't try to make something out of this that didn't exist. It's bad enough as it is. I told you: I truly cared for your mother. At one point I even thought I was in love with her. But I just didn't want to get married, to her or anyone else for that matter."

"I'm sorry, sir. It's just that this is all so hard for me to believe and to accept. You're talking about *my mother.*" He emphasized the words.

"I understand, Ray." Bob tried to sound sympathetic.

"No, you don't. But I think I understand, and though it's impossible for me to picture my mother in the situation you describe, I can see how it might have happened. You were a young, good-looking soldier, looking for sex, and there was my mother, an innocent girl. You sweet-talked her, made promises you couldn't keep, and convinced her you loved her, and she succumbed to you. You were a cad."

"No, it wasn't that way at all. You're wrong. I have to admit it now—the truth is that I really did love your mother, very much. But I did not want to get married. I couldn't for personal reasons. But we're getting off the topic. The question isn't whether I loved your mother; the question is who fathered you since it could have been either George or me. No one can be sure, Ray, and we cannot prove if I am your father or not," Bob continued.

"You're not my father," Ray replied, "and don't ever suggest that you are or might be."

"But I just explained—"

"You explained that it's possible that you may have sired me, but my father? No. George Bishop is and always has been my father, whether he planted the seeds of my being or not. He's been a better father to me than most men ever are or hope to be. Let's not get the two issues confused, Mr. Ruthers." He dropped the lighter on the table and reached for another cigarette. His throat was beginning to burn from the number of cigarettes he had smoked in the last hour.

Bob felt a lump rise in his throat. *Here*, he thought, *is a truly fine boy*. Allison and George had done a good job raising him. "I'm glad you feel the way you do," Bob said. "You have no idea how glad. Had things been different, I would have been overjoyed to call you my son-in-law. I hope that someday Lorene marries someone as nice as you and as understanding."

"Why can't Lorene and I marry anyway?" Ray asked. It was a serious question.

"Why? Isn't it obvious? Would you marry your sister?"

"Half-sister, Mr. Ruthers, and we're not even sure of that."

"Surely you can see the complications for yourself. If you two married, it would necessitate your having no children. Would you, loving Lorene as you do, deprive her of that privilege, of that joy?"

"We could adopt children."

"It's difficult to do. You'd have to show that you two were incapable of having your own. And if you were childless, how would you explain to Lorene your reasons for not having a family? Would you tell her the truth?"

"No, I couldn't. I don't know how she would feel knowing that she might be married to her half-brother. But can't we do something to find out who my biological father is?"

"We'd have to have extensive blood work done, and your mother does not want to risk your father finding out that he might not be or definitely is not your father. She loves your father, and she does not want to hurt him or jeopardize their marriage." Bob knew he was lying about Allison's position, but he was not going to leave the door open to have the blood work Allison had suggested. "So, Ray, for goodness sake, be sensible. How can you marry Lorene?"

"You've got me over a barrel, Mr. Ruthers. But what can I do?" he asked.

Once again, the waitress interrupted. She put down two BLT sandwich plates with pickle and potato salad. "Anything to drink?" she asked.

`"Nothing, thank you. The water is fine. Unless you want a drink, Ray."

Ray shook his head no and pushed the plate away. He was not hungry at all.

"What do you expect me to do?" Ray asked again.

`"You have to break it off. Tell her … tell her anything, but end it all. And the sooner the better."

"I'll try to think of something. I guess I have to. But you have to understand, I love Lorene and I want to spend the rest of my life with her."

"You won't tell her the truth, though, will you?"

"No, I won't tell that to anyone, ever. I can't. Lorene will be very hurt no matter what I tell her, but I can't hurt her with the truth. And as much as I dislike you, I can't disillusion her about her father. I love her, and I am heartbroken that I have to hurt her and lose her."

"I'm sorry, Ray, so very sorry that this all had to happen. Lorene will get over it; I know she will. And so will you," Bob said.

"I'm sorry too, sir. In one afternoon, in a few hours, my

birthright is questioned, my mother's moral fiber is impugned, and the girl I love is taken away from me." He reached out to the BLT and pushed the plate further away.

"What can I say or do?" Bob asked. "What can I do to make this easier for you?"

"Nothing, nothing at all," Ray answered. "You've said it all and done it all a long time ago." He rose to leave. "You're a man with no moral fiber."

"You make me feel terrible. You make me feel that I did something wrong." Bob tried to explain: "I didn't do any more than hundred of thousands of others in the war did. Or, I'll wager, any more than you've done yourself."

"That may be true," Ray answered, "only you did it to *my* mother." He picked up the pack of cigarettes and put them in his pocket.

"Don't leave yet, Ray. I want to say something else. Someday, someone may say the same thing to you that you've been saying to me. I hope not, but it doesn't always happen to the other man," Bob explained.

"I doubt it," Ray answered. "Some girls are meant to be loved and are by many, and some girls are meant to be loved but only by one. Your trouble was that you couldn't keep your two categories straight." Now Ray sounded angry.

"I never forced your mother," Bob answered in defense of his own position.

Ray sat down again. "Not with violence, but perhaps with words, or gestures, or hope."

"I never misled her or lied to her about my feelings."

"Did she tell you she loved you?" Ray asked. "Did you tell her you loved her?"

"Yes, we both professed love for each other, but she knew I was not going to marry her or anyone else."

"And when you knew she was pregnant and the child might be yours, did you take any responsibility?" Ray was really worked up at this point.

"She was married. She had a husband."

"So that relieved you of all responsibility? You could wash your hands of the whole thing and just walk away? Did she offer to divorce my father and marry you if the child was yours?"

"Yes, but what would you have done in my shoes?" Bob asked. "You would most likely have acted the same way."

Ray refused to answer. "Goodbye, Mr. Ruthers." He got up and started to walk out quickly.

"I'm sorry!" Bob yelled out.

"Don't be," Ray called back to him. "You really don't feel sorry for me. You don't give a damn. If you did, you wouldn't have told me all this. I feel sorry for Lorene having a father like you."

"When you finish school," Bob added, "come to my firm and see me. I think I can do something for you."

"No, thank you," Ray answered. "I don't want your charity. You've done quite enough for me already." He turned back toward the door and left rapidly. It was the last time Bob was ever to see him.

Bob sat quietly. It was all over. *Poor Lorene*, he thought. Then he said aloud, "The sins of our fathers," and drank the rest of his water.

Chapter 22

Gloria sat in the den nervously awaiting Bob's return. It was eight o'clock in the evening, and she had not heard from him all day. She couldn't imagine what had happened. He had met Ray for lunch. *Could they still be together?* she asked herself, and then she thought, *No, that's not possible. But where could Bob be? Why didn't he contact me? He knows how worried I am. This is very inconsiderate of him.* All these thoughts kept running through her mind. At 8:15 she suddenly heard his key turning in the lock, and she rushed to the front hall. Bob closed the door behind him and breathed a deep sigh. He removed his jacket and hung it in the hall closet. Then, with Gloria following alongside him continuingly asking, "Well? Well? What happened? What happened? Talk to me, Bob," he walked, heavy footed, into the den and sank into the brown leather armchair. He leaned his head against the back and stretched a hand out on each of the arms. He eyes were closed, his breathing slow and methodical. Gloria perched herself on the matching footstool adjacent to the chair. Her right hand twisted itself about her left thumb, rubbing and pulling the finger in one gesture as she continued desperately to get an answer from Bob.

"Well? Well?" she repeated over and over again, and then she added a barrage of questions: "Do you realize what time it is? Do you realize how worried I was? Why didn't you call me? How inconsiderate can you be?"

Bob didn't answer. Gloria looked at him, searching for a response, and suddenly realized how exhausted and worn he looked. She realized things could not have gone well.

"Can I get you something? A drink? Some food?" she asked.

"Nothing, thank you." He opened his eyes and looked directly into hers. "It was awful, just awful. I know I should have called you, but I couldn't. I just could not tell you over the phone what had transpired."

"What happened? Tell me now."

"I told him, Gloria. I told him everything. I think he hates me."

"I doubt he hates you, Bob. I'm sure he was upset. But didn't he understand at all?" she asked.

"Oh, he understood all right. He understood too much. He could read between the lines. He blamed me and said a number of not-very-nice things about me." Bob almost sobbed. "It was not easy to take."

"What did he blame you for? Not telling your story earlier?"

"No. He blamed me because of what I did to his mother. I abandoned her and didn't take responsibility for what might have been my child. And, if his mother truly loved me, did I lead her on? And there was more. It's too hurtful and difficult for me to repeat."

"Oh!" Gloria exclaimed simply and dropped her head in silence.

"What does *oh* mean? Have you no other comment?"

"Do you think he was wrong in what he said? I don't mean how he said it. That may not have been the most civil way to react. I mean what he said. Was he wrong?"

"You don't understand, do you?"

"Frankly, no. I do not understand running away from your

responsibility, especially since you loved this girl. Admit it. You loved her but couldn't marry her because of your parents. If she had been Jewish, would you have married her? For Pete's sake, you aren't religious now and you weren't then. Be honest with yourself. Would you have married her?"

"I don't know what I would have done." He continued to avoid answering whether he had loved Allison.

"I don't know if that's an honest answer or not. There's so much about you that I've found out lately. I never realized how self-serving you are and how much you've hidden from me all these years."

"Well, thank goodness I didn't tell Lorene," he said, changing the subject. "Considering how you and Ray feel, she never would have forgiven me."

"What will Ray do now?"

"I don't know. He didn't see why they couldn't get married anyway."

"Really?" Gloria was surprised. "He was willing to run the risk of not having children? He must be very much in love with her."

"I hope he's going to break it off with her tomorrow. They have a date. It's the last day before he leaves for Troy to go back to school."

"It will all be over soon, Bob. Tomorrow we will know what he is going to do. And remember, one possibility is that he may tell Lorene."

"Oh, no!" Bob exclaimed. "I specifically asked him not to."

"Well, if he does you will find out what Lorene's reaction will be. I won't try to guess how she will feel, although I have a gut feeling she will be less than happy and blame you."

"Where is she, by the way?"

"She's over at her friend's house. The two of them are planning their weddings."

"Well, I hope Ray breaks it off tomorrow. That's the smartest thing to do," Bob said.

"If he does," Gloria began, "you know who will be badly hurt?'

"Lorene. And I feel sorry, but she'll get over it as soon as she meets someone else."

"Is that how you felt when you left Allison? She'll get over it and so will you? No, the one damaged the most in all of this is Ray. He has to live with this secret. He has to live knowing that his father may not be his biological father. He has to live knowing that his mother had another lover. He has to give up the girl he loves. He's the one who is going to suffer the most. It's about time you stopped thinking only of yourself and what's important to you. I told you before you went that I thought what you were doing was cruel. I haven't changed my mind."

"Well, you're entitled to your opinion. I don't agree. But it will all be over soon. Ray will have to do something tomorrow night because he's leaving after that. Gloria, I am tired," he continued "I'm more than that. I'm exhausted. I don't know if I will be able to sleep, but I'm going to try. Let's go to bed."

He rose from the chair, and they walked quietly, not speaking, into the foyer and up the stairs. Once in the bedroom they undressed slowly and prepared for bed. Gloria finished first and sat watching Bob as he moved noiselessly about, donning first his pajama pants and then the top.

"I imagine you are condemning yourself," she said. "I know you did what you thought was right and best."

"I'm not thinking about tonight at the moment. I'm thinking of twenty-six years ago," he answered. "But I appreciate your trying to pacify the situation."

"What you did can't be undone," she said. "This is no time to regret."

"You are right, of course," he replied. "But it's easier said than done."

He switched off the overhead light, leaving only the nightstand lamp lit, and lay on his back staring at the partially darkened ceiling. His thoughts couldn't be pinpointed. They were fleetingly covering twenty-six years of his life and questioning why and how.

"Are you going to sleep now?" Gloria asked.

"In a few minutes," he replied. "Why do you ask?"

"There's something I have to say. I said it earlier, but I don't know if it really registered with you. Bob, you are a different man from the one I married. Maybe I just didn't see it then, but the man you are today I do not like. You have become self-centered and indifferent to the feelings of others. You have displayed characteristics that make me question your morals. In short, I am unhappy about the man I see before me. I love you, and you have many fine qualities. But our relationship is going to change. It's changing because I'm changing. I don't feel the same way anymore. Don't misunderstand me; I'm not asking for a divorce. Things may be different when Lorene marries and is out of the house. But for now, though our situation will remain the same, our relationship will not. Now is not the time to discuss how the relationship will change, but I just felt I had to tell you. I could not pretend that everything was okay."

"I understand," he answered. "I really do. I felt this coming. I could feel the difference in your attitude, in your warmth. I guess I don't blame you. But I want you to know one thing—I *do love* you." He emphasized the words. "I have always loved you and I always will."

Tears came to Gloria's eyes. She knew he loved her, and she felt a pang of guilt that she could no longer have the same deep feelings for him. All she could say was, "Thank you."

"Good night, Gloria. Sleep well." He reached over and turned off the lamp, leaving the room in complete darkness.

"Good night," she replied, and she rolled over onto her left side so that her back was facing Bob.

How long Bob lay there contemplating his life he did not know, but it seemed as if only a few minutes later the first beam of sunlight filtered across the ceiling, illuminating the room in a gray light. It was six o'clock, and a new day had dawned.

Chapter 23

Ray sat for hours trying to decide what was the right thing to do. He didn't come out of his bedroom for the remainder of the day after meeting with Bob. Allison thought he was sick, but he reassured her that he was okay, just tired. The next day he left the house early and went to a library in town, where he knew could sit and think while pretending to read. He realized he was meeting Lorene that evening, and he had to have an answer by then.

What are the choices? he thought. *I can tell Lorene, and together we can decide if we want to take the chance. It is a fifty-fifty chance, so the odds aren't with or against us. If I do that I will destroy any relationship Lorene has with her father. And what if she says she won't take the chance? Then I've destroyed a family and nothing good has come out of it. I can say nothing and just go on as if nothing happened. But is that fair to Lorene? No, I can't do that. I will have to end our relationship. But how? I can do it gradually. Go off to school and not contact her for two weeks, then let three or four weeks go by? Each letter or phone call would be more impersonal. That might let her down more easily. Would I like that if the tables were turned?* he thought. *I don't think so. Both Lorene and I prefer honesty. I will have to tell her, outright, that it is over. A clean, fast break will be difficult for her to*

handle, but it's best. Like quitting smoking, you just have to stop. Lorene
will want to know why. What should I tell her? I can't say I don't love
her; that would be a lie. I just have to make up a bunch of excuses.

Once he had decided on the path to take, he began to concentrate
on what excuses he would make. He dreaded the prospect of the
entire evening.

Contrary to Ray's predicament, Lorene was home all day
eagerly awaiting her evening date with Ray. She washed and curled
her hair and polished her nails. She carefully selected the dress she
was going to wear. She wanted everything to be perfect. This was to
be their last date for a while since Ray was leaving for college. They
had discussed the problems they would have seeing each other. Ray
needed the weekends to study, and Lorene's parents would not let
her go to Troy and stay in a hotel. Ray promised that he would drive
down if he got a free weekend. Otherwise, they would have to wait
for Thanksgiving when he would have four days off.

Lorene was ready early. She sat in the living room where she
could look out the window and see when Ray arrived. She noted
that there was a beautiful full moon and a sky full of stars. It was
a perfect night. It was a romantic night, and Lorene felt romantic.

When Ray pulled up, he honked the horn instead of parking
and walking up to the house to pick Lorene up. *This is the first step*
in changing my behavior, he thought.

Lorene saw the car parked at the curb. She waited a few minutes
for Ray to get out and come up to the house. Instead, she heard a
second insistent honk of the horn. "I'm leaving now. See you later,"
she called out to her parents as she bolted out the door, wondering
why Ray was sitting in his car.

Lorene opened the door on the passenger side and slid onto

the seat. She felt that something was wrong. Ray did not get out to help her into the car as he usually did. He didn't lean over to give her a kiss. He didn't put an arm around her, and his greeting was less than warm.

"Hi," he said as he started the car.

"Hi, yourself. What's wrong?" She had never seen him in such a mood.

"What makes you think something is wrong?" he asked.

"You're so distant, and you're not acting like yourself."

"It's just one of my moody days," he replied.

"What are you talking about?" Lorene asked. "I've never seen you moody."

"Well, you have now."

"Ray, you're scaring me. What's wrong? You're like a different person. Come on, honey, lighten up. Let's make the most of tonight. It's the last night in a long time that we will be together. Do you like this color of nail polish?" she asked, trying to change the tone of things as she held her hand up in front of his face.

"It's nice."

"Is that all you have to say? What's with you, Ray? Are you nervous about going back to school? Are you upset about having to leave?" Lorene was fruitlessly searching for answers and feeling completely frustrated. "It's such a beautiful night. It's such a romantic night, and with that gorgeous moon," she said, "we should do something special."

"How about going to the Italian restaurant?" Ray asked. "The food is good, and it's quiet there. I want to talk to you."

"Okay, if that's what you want." Lorene was disappointed, but she didn't want to argue with him, not on this last night they would have together for a while. The Italian restaurant was not what she had in mind as being romantic.

He drove quietly the few blocks to Central Avenue. The street was lined with stores, all closed now. There were two or three restaurants in the four blocks that made up the center of town, as well as an ice cream parlor where the high school kids stopped on their way home for a soda or sundae. There was also a jewelry store, a dry cleaner, a beauty parlor, a shoemaker, a drug store, and many others that Lorene spotted as they drove past them to the end of the strip, where the Italian restaurant was located. They called it a restaurant, but it was more of a pizza parlor. Ray found a parking spot. No words had been spoken while they drove through town or while they entered the restaurant. They seated themselves in a booth near the entrance. The restaurant had pictures of Italian cities and countryside on the walls, and the décor was red and white, including red-and-white plaid tablecloths so typical of Italian restaurants..

The waitress came over and handed them menus. "Take your time," she said. "While you make up your mind, can I bring you something to drink?"

"I'll have a beer," Ray said and then turned his attention to the menu.

"Ray, I'm here too," Lorene said, and then to the waitress, "I'll have a Diet Coke." Lorene was confused and upset. Ray had never ignored her before. On the contrary, he had always been overly caring and thoughtful. She felt something was terribly wrong, but she didn't know what or why.

"I'll be back for your order," the waitress said as she walked away.

"I don't know what I want. Do you? What do you think about getting a pizza?"

`"I guess that's okay," he said." I'm not really that hungry."

"You're not anything tonight, Ray," she replied. "I don't know what to make of you."

"I have a lot on my mind."

"I knew it. You're worried about going back to school." Lorene sighed in relief. She was sure she had the answer to Ray's strange behavior.

"That's not it," he said. "There is something else bothering me."

At that moment, the waitress appeared with a beer and a Coke. "Have you decided what you want to eat?" she asked.

"We're not very hungry," Ray answered. "I think it will just be drinks."

"Ray!" Lorene protested as the waitress walked away.

"Please, Lorene," Ray pleaded. "I have to talk to you. It's very important, and I just don't know how to start."

"What in the world are you talking about?" she asked.

"Lorene, I have something to tell you. I want you to listen carefully, and I hope you will understand." He stopped for a moment to take a drink of beer. "I have been giving a great deal of thought to us, our relationship, and our plans, and it scares me."

`"What do you mean it scares you?" she asked. Lorene was now very nervous. She didn't know where the conversation was going.

He blurted it out." I still have a year of school, and I have to concentrate if I'm going to pass. I'm not the best of students, and the work is hard. I have no job and nothing on the horizon; it may be months after I graduate before I find employment. So I won't be able to support a wife. I love you, Lorene, but I think we acted prematurely. I don't think—no, that's wrong—I *know* I am not ready for a commitment to anyone. And you still have years of college ahead of you. You should continue and get your degree before you think of settling down."

"I can't believe I'm hearing this. I can't believe what you are saying." Lorene was stunned.

"I'm saying that I think we should break it off. Neither of us is ready."

"But," she argued, "we discussed all this. We agreed that we would be willing to struggle together, that we could make it work. What changed your mind?" At this point her eyes were filled with tears; she was on the verge of crying. "What happened, Ray?"

"We were not realistic. We were behaving like children, not mature adults. I told you, I'm not ready; it's not fair to you or me. Now, if you don't mind, I'd like to take you home." He signaled the waitress and called, "Check, please."

"Just like that?" Now the tears began to flow. "I can't believe this. Just like that you're telling me it's over. I thought we loved each other. How can you do this? How could you?" Lorene began to sob.

"Please, Lorene. Try to understand. This is best for both of us. When the year is up, if we still feel the same way, we can always get together again. Please try to understand," he pleaded.

"No, I don't understand. I don't understand at all." She grabbed the paper napkin to wipe the tears from her face, but they kept coming. She couldn't stop crying.

The waitress arrived with the check. Ray reached into his pocket and pulled out some bills. "Here," he said. "The rest is for you."

"Thank you," she said as she walked away.

Turning to Lorene, he said, "Please don't cry. It breaks my heart to see you this way. I am truly sorry, Lorene. And I don't want to hurt you. I just wish you could understand and see it my way. But that's the way it has to be. I'll take you home now. I want to get home early tonight so I have time to say goodbye to my folks. I'm leaving early in the morning."

They walked quietly back to the car and drove silently back to Lorene's house.

"Good night, Lorene," Ray said. "And I am truly sorry. You can't imagine how sorry I really am. I am heartbroken. But it just could not work out now. Maybe someday you will understand."

"I suppose you want your silver dollar back," Lorene said as she reached into her purse to get it. She was still crying, and the words came out between sobs.

"No, please, I want you to keep the silver dollar. I really do. I have to go now, Lorene. It's time for me to head home."

Lorene got out of the car and ran up the path. She opened the front door and rushed to her bedroom, slamming the door behind her. She then threw herself on her bed and sobbed.

Gloria and Bob had been sitting in the den reading. They heard the front door open and close and Lorene's footsteps as she ran up the stairs. They could hear her sobs until they heard the door slam.

"What did Ray say to her?" Gloria asked, not expecting an answer. Bob was silent. "I think I'd best go to her." She placed a bookmark on the page she was reading and put the book on the cocktail table. Then she got up and went up the stairs. Bob followed silently behind her.

"Lorene," Gloria called out. "What's wrong?"

"Go away. I don't want to talk to anyone. Just leave me alone," she sobbed.

"Lorene, darling, please let me come in," Gloria pleaded.

"Mom, I don't want to see anyone now. Just leave me alone."

"No, I will not. I'm coming in." To Bob, she said, "You wait here. This is for a mother and daughter."

Bob was happy to be excluded from what he knew was not going to be a pleasant situation. He retreated to the master bedroom, sat on the bed, and wondered how Ray had handled it. Obviously, he had broken up with Lorene, and she was taking it very badly. *She'll get over it*, he thought. *God forgive me for bringing her so much pain.*

Gloria opened her daughter's bedroom door to find her lying on her bed in the dark, sobbing hysterically. She walked over, put her arms around her, and hugged her tightly. "I'm here for you darling. I'm here. Talk to me," she whispered.

"Oh, Mom." She could barely get the words out between her sobs. "It's over. He broke it off."

"Oh, darling. I am so sorry for you. Did he say why?"

"Only that he wasn't ready to make a commitment now. He has to finish school and get a job. He also said that I should finish my degree. He said other things like not having time to study, not being able to come down to see me, and lots more. He also said that in a year when he has graduated and working that we might get back together." Lorene had gotten back some control. No longer was she sobbing.

"It's easy for me to say," Gloria said, "but it will all work out, darling. Believe me, it will all work out." She patted her daughter's head and ran her hand through her hair. "I know how you feel. I felt the same way when my first love walked out on me."

"Somebody dumped you?"

"Oh, yes. It was in high school. But I thought I was in love. It wasn't like your relationship with Ray, but it hurt just as much."

Gloria's heart broke for her daughter, and she was angry at the same time that Bob had caused all this. She knew that he, too, was devastated at the pain he had caused his daughter, but she realized that, at the same time, he was relieved that it was all over. Once again he had been able to deflect consequences from himself.

"How did you get over it?" Lorene asked.

"Time is a wonderful healer, darling. And it helped that I met a football player and was infatuated with him. It didn't last long, but it helped me to get over the lost love. You should have seen this football player. He was gorgeous and built like Adonis."

Gloria laughed as she wiped a tear from Lorene's cheek, and she was happy to see that her story brought a smile to Lorene as well.

"That's better," Gloria said. "A smile is better than tears. Honey,

I guarantee you will begin to feel better. Tomorrow it won't hurt as much, and the next day it will hurt a little less. And each day will be better and better until all the hurt will be gone." She hugged Lorene again and they remained there, locked in each other's arms.

Outside, Ray sat in his car. He just could not get himself to drive away. He struck a match and lit a cigarette, took a deep puff, and blew the smoke out slowly. He hated himself for hurting Lorene the way he had. He really did love her, but what choice did he have? He could not tell his parents what he knew. How could he hurt his father that way? How devastating that would be for his mother. He couldn't do that to them. He had no choice but to break up with Lorene. He had spent hours thinking of how he could end the relationship without inflicting pain on her, but he could think of no way. His final decision to just cut it off, end it quickly, was the kindest way to handle it, he believed. He cursed Bob for burdening him with the devastating secret, and he knew that he would have to live with the hurt he had inflicted for the rest of his life. Having finished the cigarette, he crushed it in the ashtray. He turned to look at the house, and then his eyes moved to the second-floor window that he knew was Lorene's room.

"Goodbye, Lorene," he said to himself. "I really do love you."

He started the car and drove away, taking one last look back as he did so.

CHAPTER

Chapter 24

Bob and Gloria rose at about the same time. Both had had restless nights, both concerned with how Lorene was going to handle things. Gloria headed into the bathroom, and Bob waited his turn. When she emerged, she said, "All yours," and she left the room to go downstairs and into the kitchen. Everything was quiet in Lorene's room as she walked past the closed door. *I hope she's sleeping*, Gloria thought. *She has to be exhausted.* She walked down the carpeted stairs quietly so as not to disturb Lorene. Once in the kitchen she inserted a filter into the basket of the coffee maker. Then she measured out eight spoonfuls of coffee and put them into the basket. Finally, she poured eight cups of water into the rear of the coffee maker and turned it on. Almost immediately the coffee began to filter through and flow into the coffee pot. That being done, she turned her attention to the rest of the breakfast. She removed a bagel from the refrigerator and popped it into the toaster. Next came the cream cheese, which she put on the kitchen table. After putting a place setting on the table, she removed the toasted bagel and placed it on the plate. Next, she poured a cup of coffee into Bob's favorite mug, one Lorene had given him for Father's Day that said "Best dad," and put that on the table too.

Finally, she poured a glass of orange juice and placed it on the table.

When Bob came into the kitchen just minutes later, he was fully dressed, ready for work. It was seven o'clock, and he had time to catch the 7:45 train into the city. A number of his friends and acquaintances made the same train. They sat in the smoking section, turned the seats to face one another, and played cards. Usually, they played gin rummy. Bob said it made the trip go faster and the camaraderie was very enjoyable. He sat down at the breakfast table and remarked, "Just what I ordered," in as cheerful a way as he could. "Thank you."

"You're welcome," Gloria said icily. "I'm not sitting with you while you eat," she added. "I'm going to get dressed so I can drive you to the station. The newspaper is there for you."

Bob sat quietly eating his breakfast and scanning the paper. He was in no mood to read. Gloria's attitude was very clear. The atmosphere was more than cool; it was cold. He wondered how long Gloria would keep it up. He wondered if he could do something to alleviate the tension. *Maybe I should bring her flowers*, he thought. He knew he was responsible, but he still felt that he was right to handle it as he had. He ate the bagel slowly, one small bite at a time. As he consumed the last bite and the final sip of coffee, Gloria came back in the room. She was wearing a cotton sundress with large red and yellow flowers printed on the skirt. She was summery looking, and he, in tie and jacket, was a sharp contrast.

"You look lovely," Bob complimented her. "Is that a new dress? I don't remember it."

"Thanks," she replied. "No, it's not new. I guess you didn't notice it before."

"Maybe not, but I should have. You really do look lovely."

"Time to go," she said, ignoring his remark. She put the dishes, silver, and mug in the sink. "I'll wash them when I get back."

They walked to the door silently. The car was parked in the driveway, and Gloria slid into the driver's seat while Bob positioned himself in the front passenger seat. She backed out carefully and headed up the street to West Broadway. Then she cut across to Central Avenue and took another side street to the station. There was no conversation during the ride. Bob felt very uncomfortable. When they arrived, she pulled to a stop, and Bob opened his door and stepped out. There was no "Have a good day" or kiss goodbye. He got out, and she drove off immediately. All he could hope for was that she would be different by dinnertime. Somehow, though, he doubted it. *Maybe flowers are a good idea*, he thought. *A dozen roses may soften her up.*

Gloria turned on the radio as she drove home. She needed to hear some lively music, something to lift her spirits. She knew the songs and hummed along with the music. It made her feel a little bit better. She pulled the car into the driveway, got out, locked the door, and headed into the house. Things were quiet, so she knew Lorene was still sleeping. She went into the kitchen, where her first task was to wash the items in the sink. It only took a few minutes. Then she poured herself a cup of coffee; it was still hot because the pot had stayed on for a period of time. She sat down and opened the paper to the puzzle page. She loved doing the crossword puzzle and tried to finish it each morning. She realized this was not *The New York Times* but a puzzle in the local paper. It wasn't as difficult, but she got great satisfaction, nevertheless, from finishing it. She was working on it for about one half hour when suddenly the phone rang.

It's eight thirty, she thought. *Who would be calling at this hour?*

She lifted the receiver of the harvest-green wall phone, picked to match the appliances.

"Hello?"

"Oh, Gloria. It's me, Gladys. I'm sorry to call so early, but I know you're up and I just had to talk to someone. Did I get you at a bad time?"

"No, not at all. Just having coffee and doing the puzzle. But what's wrong? You sound terrible. Are you okay?" Gloria was very concerned but knew that Gladys had a tendency to overreact to things. She could exaggerate situations to the point that it seemed that it was life or death. She took everything so seriously that Gloria never knew when it was a real tragedy or something that could be handled easily.

"It's Eileen, Gloria. I have some very bad news."

"Bad news? About Eileen? What happened? What can I do?" Gloria asked sincerely. " Do you want me to come over?" Gloria was always the first to offer help when a friend was in trouble.

"Thanks for the offer," Gladys responded "There's nothing you can do. It's terrible and I'm very upset. Poor Eileen"

"What do you mean *poor Eileen*? Is she all right?"

"Yes and no."

"What does that mean? Either she's okay or she's not," Gloria countered.

"It's just that she had something wrong. It's why she lost the baby. She had a large cyst."

"I see," Gloria said. "I gather they removed the cyst?"

"She had a number of cysts."

"Gladys, stop beating around the bush. Tell me what happened." Gloria was getting impatient.

"Oh, Gloria, they had to do a hysterectomy. A *hysterectomy!* Can you imagine? She's so young. And this means she will never be able to have a child! I am devastated. I don't know what to do, what to say, or how to handle it."

"I'm so very, very sorry," Gloria said. "I know you have to be very upset, but Eileen—she's the one most affected. How is she taking it?"

"She seems to be taking it okay, better than I am, I think. Does this mean I'll never be a grandmother?" Gladys started to cry as she said the words.

Gloria reached for a pack of cigarettes, pulled one out, and lit it. She smoked filtered Chesterfields and felt that smoking calmed her nerves. *Why do people always think of themselves first?* she thought and then said, "Calm down, Gladys. The important thing is Eileen's health. How long will she be in the hospital?"

"About a week, I think, until she recovers from the surgery."

"Okay, deal with first things first. You visit her and assure her everything will be okay." Gloria was always the level-headed one. "I know this is a big blow to you, but you can't let Eileen see that. It's a bigger blow to her. When she's all well and back on her feet, you can discuss the future with her." Gloria's suggestions were logical.

"Oh, her attitude seems wonderful. She's already talking about other alternatives. She says she and Peter want to have a child and this is not going to stop them. She mentioned the possibility of adoption."

"Good for her. I'm glad to hear she has a positive attitude," Gloria added. "You know, Gladys, there are many ways today to have a child, and adoption is just one of them. Don't worry; you will be a grandmother someday." And then with a sudden thought, Gloria said, "I just had an idea."

"Adoption today is very difficult," Gladys continued, ignoring Gloria's mention of an idea. "It's almost impossible to get a child. I'm sure they will think it through and come up with something. Gloria, thank you so much for being my sounding board. I just had to get it all off my chest." Gladys had calmed down and truly appreciated her friend's advice.

"Gladys," Gloria said, "I may have the perfect answer. I told you I have an idea."

"What are you talking about?"

Gloria continued, "I'm so excited. I just happened to remember—I know someone who is pregnant and willing to give up her child for adoption!"

"You do?" Gladys was shocked.

"Yes, it won't be for another six or seven months now, but I know she is putting the child up for adoption. I think I can get her together with Eileen, and they can make the arrangements."

"Oh, that would be a miracle. That would be a prayer answered. Get right on it, Gloria!"

"I will. I have a good feeling about this; this would be a win-win situation for everyone. I'll get back to you the next time I speak with her."

Gladys didn't even ask who it was. She was ecstatic. All she could say was, "Thank you! Thank you!"

"I'll talk to you tomorrow," Gloria said and hung up the phone.

She ground out her cigarette in the multicolored ceramic ashtray Lorene had made for her when she was a teenager in camp.

Life goes on, she thought. *But sometimes it is so difficult.*

With that thought in mind, she left the kitchen and started up the stairs. Lorene's door was still closed, but she thought she heard some movement inside.

"Lorene," she called out, "I'm here." She opened the door and went in. *It's time to comfort my daughter*, she thought. *She's the one who needs me now.*

Chapter 25

FORTY YEARS LATER, 2006

Lorene had risen, showered, and dressed and was busily putting the bedspread back on her bed in her three-bedroom ranch house in Valley Stream on Long Island. The house was just the right size for Lorene; her husband, Roger; and their two children, Rita and David. She and Roger had met in college, and they married when both graduated. They had had a good life, and Lorene loved her home. She called it comfortable and warm. The only thing missing in the small rancher was a den. Roger desperately wanted to move to a larger house and had picked out a home in a new development a few blocks away, but Lorene was so content and so unhappy with the idea of moving that Roger gave in and Lorene compromised, agreeing to enlarge their present home by adding a den off of the kitchen. It was wood paneled in pecky cypress, and in the center was a large wood-burning fireplace framed in stone. Lorene admitted that the addition was wonderful and spent many hours in the room.

Lorene sighed as she put the finishing touches on the flowered bedspread on the king-sized bed. The small house now seemed so very big to her. The children were grown and on their own, and she was alone still mourning the loss of her husband six months earlier. He had had a sudden, massive heart attack. One moment he was sitting watching television with her, and the next he was slumped over and struggling to breathe. The ambulance responded very quickly, but there was nothing anyone could do. Everyone said he was too young for such a heart attack, but Lorene knew it ran in his family. His father and brother had died while in their forties. Now, Lorene was trying to get her life back together. She had told herself that she had to go back to her normal routine and start living life again. She opened her purse and took out two theater tickets. *Roger and I bought these tickets for* Sing Along *a year in advance*, she thought. They were so difficult to get because the show had won three Tony Awards, one for best musical, one for best direction, and one for best actress. *We both so looked forward to seeing the show*, she remembered. She had called the box office and tried in vain to return one ticket after Roger passed away, but there was a no-returns policy. She had offered the ticket to girlfriends, but each had a different excuse for why they could not make it that day. *I'll hand it in at the box office when I get there. I'm sure they will be able to sell it. There's no point in it going to waste*, she thought. *Roger, dear, I will have to see it without you, but it won't be easy. I will picture you there beside me.* Then she wondered, *How can I go to a show in the city by myself? How will I do it?* She took a deep breath and resolved that this was something she was going to do. It was something she *had* to do.

"Today will be the first step," she told herself.

She dressed in a tailored pantsuit realizing that the theater is usually cool and a jacket was necessary. When she was ready, she went outside, clicked the remote to open the garage door, got in the car, and backed it onto the driveway. Another click and the door closed. It was only a few blocks to the Valley Stream station.

She knew she was catching a noon train, and a few minutes after she parked, the train arrived. The ride was uneventful. The train was almost empty, and she sat in a window seat and watched the landscape as they headed for New York. Once they entered the tunnel, she knew they were almost there. When the train stopped, she exited and headed for the subway, where she took the train to Forty-Second Street. From there it was only a few blocks' walk to Forty-Fifth Street. The theater was just a block west of Broadway. She was very early, but she didn't care.

When she arrived at the box office, she took out Roger's ticket.

"I have an extra ticket that I cannot use," she told the ticket seller, noting the "Sold Out" sign. "Maybe someone will want it."

He thanked her for turning it in and said, "This will make someone very happy."

Noting that the theater was open, she headed inside. The usher guided her to her seat, which was fifth row center, and handed her the program. *The seat to my left would have been Roger's*, she mused as she became absorbed with the program. She read every page, every biography, and every ad, and she didn't look up until the house lights dimmed and the overture began. At the last moment, just as the curtain was going up, a man sat down next to her. Lorene loved the show and was mesmerized by the costumes and special effects. It was a wonderful, funny musical, and for the duration of the performance, she forgot her other problems and was completely involved in the actions on stage. When the curtain fell on Act I and the house lights came on, she rose so she could walk a little during the intermission. As she started to pass the gentleman to her left, she turned to face him. He looked up in amazement.

"Lorene?" he questioned. "Is it you?"

Lorene took a long, hard look. Forty years had altered his appearance but there was no mistaking the voice and the face. He was balding and had put on weight.

"Ray? Ray Bishop?"

"It's me. Lorene, it's so good to see you!" he said enthusiastically. "You don't know how many times I've thought of you, wondering how you were and what you were doing."

"Ray, I really don't want anything to do with you. You hurt me very badly years ago. I'm not looking to be hurt again."

"I can explain," he said. "Just give me a chance. The coincidence that I got this seat next to you must mean something."

"I don't know what to say," she replied. "You broke my heart."

"We can't talk here," Ray noted. "Please, come with me after the show. Come for a drink. We have to talk. There is so much I have to tell you."

"I don't know. I'm wary of having anything to do with you again," she said.

"Just give me a chance, please. I promise I can explain everything."

Deep down in her heart, Lorene still had feelings for Ray. *You never forget your first love*, she thought.

"I don't know. I don't know if I can trust you."

"Please," he pleaded. "I guarantee you won't be sorry. Give me a chance to explain."

"All right. I'll go with you for a drink, for old times' sake. But just a drink, and that's it."

At that moment, the house lights began to dim and the overture started. The second act was beginning. Lorene sat down in her seat. Ray reached over and took her hand in his.

It feels good, she thought as memories of the past flashed past her, but she quickly pulled her hand back. *I can't be hurt again*, she thought. *I won't let it happen. But what harm can there be in having a drink? Just a drink and nothing more.* Then her attention was drawn to the stage and, once again, she became absorbed and didn't think about the man sitting next to her.

Chapter 26

Ray led her to a restaurant bar a block away. They were seated opposite each other in a booth.

"You look wonderful," he said.

"Not really," she replied. "I've gotten old."

"Not to me."

The waiter appeared with a drink menu.

"I don't need that," Ray said. "I'll have a scotch and soda. How about you, Lorene?"

"A whiskey sour for me."

The waiter left for the bar, and Lorene commented, "Not drinking beer anymore?"

He laughed. "I'm a big boy now," he joked. "And I see you're not drinking Coke anymore."

She laughed too. "I'm a big girl now," she said. "Now, on a serious note, it's been forty years since we've seen each other. Our relationship ended badly. We just met again accidentally, and yet you seem to be coming on to me. Why? I don't want to be hurt again. Besides, won't your wife be upset? It's not very nice of you to make a pass at another woman when you're married. I assume you're married."

"I'm divorced. I have been for five years now. But what about you? Are you a married woman having drinks with a single man?"

"My husband passed away six months ago. It was his seat you were sitting in in the theater."

"Oh, I'm so sorry, Lorene. What happened?"

"A massive coronary."

"Did you have a good life with him?"

"Yes, we were very happy. We have a house in Valley Stream and two wonderful grown children, Rita and David. Everything was wonderful until he was suddenly taken away."

"I'm so sorry you lost your husband, but I'm so happy you have had a good life. I thought about you often and worried about what had become of you. I felt terrible about the way things ended."

"What about you? Why were you divorced?" Lorene wanted to steer the conversation away from the past.

"It wasn't a happy marriage, and I stayed until my son was old enough. I met her on a rebound from you, and it was a mistake."

Lorene was shocked. "I am so sorry, Ray. But since you felt that way about me, why did you break up with me and why didn't you contact me when you finished school?"

"I had to break up with you, and I couldn't contact you later. I'll explain. But first I have to know something: are your parents well?"

"That seems like a strange question. What does it have to do with your explanation?" she asked.

"You'll understand in a minute. Tell me, please, are your parents well?"

"My father passed away two years ago. He had cancer. Mother moved to a retirement community in Florida. But they were divorced right after I got married. But why is it important for you to know?

"I was not able to tell you anything while your father and mine were still alive."

"I am completely confused. From what you said I assume your father also passed away?" It was a statement and a question.

"Yes, my father also passed away. He had a bad fall and hit his head, and it killed him. My mother is still in the house in New Jersey."

At that moment, the waiter appeared with their drinks and a bowl of chips.

"Cheers," Ray said, and he clicked his glass against Lorene's. "And here's to the renewal of a wonderful relationship." He took a sip of his drink and then continued. "Lorene, there is something you should know. I couldn't tell you forty years ago, and I know I hurt you badly. But I had no choice. I never thought I would have the opportunity or be able to tell you this. But at least you will know why I acted as I did."

"What is it?" Lorene could not imagine what he had to say.

"I didn't walk out on you. I was forced to."

"Forced? Who forced you?" Lorene was skeptical.

"Your father."

"I don't understand. My father was dead set against our plans, but there is no way he could force you. I had told him that we were both of age and I was going ahead with our plans whether he agreed or not. Was there something in your background that he was blackmailing you about?"

"No, of course not, and of course you wouldn't understand. Your father did not want you to know why he was opposed to our relationship. He didn't tell you, but he told me."

"This is all unbelievable. I never dreamed he had a reason other than the ones he gave me. I can't imagine why he would hide his real reason, especially since I pleaded with him to explain his objection. When did he tell you what his reason was?"

"It's a long story and one your father never wanted you to know and one my mother never wanted my father to know. But they are both gone now, and I think it's important that you hear the truth. It may hurt to hear this, but for your sake and mine I think it's imperative that you do hear it."

"You have me completely confused. What in the world are you talking about? How are both our fathers involved? They didn't even know each other."

"After I tell you this, if you don't believe me, you can confirm it with your mother. But I assure you every word is the truth."

Ray began to tell the story from the very beginning. He described the love Lorene's father and his mother had for each other and that he had confirmed this with his mother after his father died. He explained the uncertainty of who fathered him. He said that when they started dating and the relationship got serious, her father wanted them to break up because it was possible they were related. "Your father was unwilling to do any testing," Ray said. "Also, the testing back then was not accurate. There was no DNA testing at that time. Finally, when he couldn't convince you to break up with me and when all else failed, your dad met with me, told me the story, and told me I had to break it off. Your dad, Lorene, did not want you to know the story. He was afraid you would be angry with him and you wouldn't understand. He loved you dearly and didn't want anything to ruin his relationship with you. Since it was possible we were related, a marriage was impossible. I couldn't tell you the truth; I promised your dad I would not tell you. So I just broke it off in the best way I knew how. Can you ever forgive me for hurting you so much?"

Lorene was stunned. She couldn't believe what she was hearing.

"Are you saying that your mother and my father were in love? And that they may have had a child together? That you are that child?"

Ray was nodding his head yes after each of her questions. He could imagine how difficult it had to be for her to accept what he was saying. He remembered how he had felt when Lorene's dad had told him the story.

"This is unbelievable. You're saying that my father didn't marry your mother, even though they were in love and even though she was pregnant?"

"That's right. He chose to believe my dad had impregnated my mother. And he may have. We don't know."

"He was right: I would not have understood. It's interesting—I sensed a difference in my parents' relationship, and I wondered why. Now I know. I'm sure my mother didn't understand either. I wonder if it had anything to do with their divorce. You must have hated my father, and I wouldn't blame you."

"*Hate* isn't the right word. I was devastated. My life had blown up in my face, and I was forced to lie to, lose, and hurt the one person I loved the most, along with facing the fact that my father may not be my father."

Lorene was listening intently. "Then you are saying that you did not want to break up with me? You really wanted to marry me?"

"That's exactly right. I loved you then, and I have always loved you."

Lorene began to cry. She didn't know whether she hated her father for causing her so much pain or if she understood his predicament. She was sure that at eighteen she would not have understood.

"Ray, I have to digest all of this. I am not questioning what you are telling me, though you have to admit it doesn't sound very realistic."

"It's the truth, every word. You can confirm it with my mother or yours. The most important thing, though, Lorene, is that I love you." He reached across the table and took her hand in his. "How could I be so lucky to find you and find out that you are not married now? In my wildest dreams I never thought there would be a possibility that you and I could be together again. I hope you still have some feelings for me. I hope I'm not coming on too strong and making a fool of myself."

"Oh, Ray," she replied. "You're bowling me over. Yes, I still have feelings for you. I was madly in love with you when I was eighteen, and a girl never forgets her first true love. At the moment I don't know how I feel. After all, you may be my half-brother."

"We can settle that for once and for all. Today there are DNA tests. Are you willing to take one?" he asked.

"Why?" she asked. "Our relationship is over."

"Not for me," he replied, "and I hope I can convince you that it's not over for you. We can revive what we had. It's not too late. We are both free to do whatever we want. Please, Lorene. Let's take the test and find out. Are we brother and sister, or are we lovers?"

"I'm not sure. Think of the ramifications. If my father is your father, how would you feel having lived your life accepting another man as your father? How would I feel knowing my father had a son and never acknowledged him and was not there for your mother? And what difference would it actually make?"

"What do you mean 'what difference would it make'?" he asked.

"When we were young, we would have wanted a family. We couldn't do that, not knowing if we were related. But Ray, we are well past the stage of having children. What difference does it make if we are related or not?"

"How would you feel making love to your brother?" he asked.

"Half-brother," she responded quickly.

"As much as I love you, I don't think I would be comfortable making love to my half-sister, and I don't think you would be with your half-brother. I still think it's important that we find out. Because," he added, "I want to make love to you. I have always loved you, Lorene, and the most wonderful thing in the world that could happen to me is to find out that George Bishop is my father."

"And I love you," she replied. "Okay, let's do it. Let's find out the truth. Let's find out if we are related or strangers."

Chapter 27

It had been three weeks since Lorene and Ray had submitted to DNA testing. In the interim, they continued to date. They did all the things they had done when they were young. They went to the stock car races, they went fishing, they ate Chinese and Italian food, and they laughed and had fun. With each date, their feelings grew stronger. However, they both refused to have an intimate relationship until they had the DNA results. Lorene knew that she still loved Ray and was nervous about the test results. If he was her half-brother, the relationship might change. Ray, too, was nervous about the results and was sorry he had insisted on the testing. Did he really care if she was his half-sister? As Lorene had pointed out, they weren't going to have children.

Each day Lorene rushed to the mailbox as soon as the mail had arrived. The box stood at the foot of her driveway and had a little red arm that the mailman stood in an upright position to indicate that he had been there and had left something. Lorene received a lot of mail, most of it what she called junk mail, so the arm was up almost daily. Each day when Lorene looked out the window and saw the red arm standing upright, she immediately rushed out in hopes that the results of the test would be there. Every time she left disappointed. They had gone to a local hospital in Queens to have the tests done, which was what Lorene's doctor had recommended. Lorene had been nervous about taking the tests, not knowing what to expect, but it turned out to be easier than she thought. They did what they called a buccal smear. With a small brush they collected sample cells from inside her cheek. The lab technician hadn't said how long it would take to get the results, but she thought that three weeks was long enough. Ray, too, was impatient and checked with Lorene daily. He had not heard anything either. That all changed on a sunny Thursday afternoon. Lorene went to the mailbox, and there was the letter. She knew it immediately. It was an official-looking envelope with the hospital's return address. She took it out and went into the house and into the den. She placed the letter on the end table. She didn't want to open it. She wanted to know what it said, and yet she did not want to know. She was afraid of what it might say. She never thought she could have such happiness again after Roger had died, and now that she found it she was frightened she might lose it. She loved Ray, and he loved her. Did anything else matter? She sat there, staring at the envelope. She wondered if Ray had gotten his letter. Finally she picked up the phone and dialed.

After two rings, he answered. "Hello?"

"Ray, I got the letter."

"Did you open it?"

`"No. I couldn't. I'm afraid of what it might say. I want you here with me when I find out. Did you get your letter?"

"Don't know. I have to check my box. I'll do that and get right out to the island. I'll be there in about an hour."

"Good. I'll be on pins and needles, but I want you with me when we read it."

The next hour seemed like five. Lorene paced the floor. She

smoked three cigarettes. She ran to the window every time she heard a car hoping it was Ray.

Ray lived in a lovely two-bedroom apartment in Queens, New York, on Forest Hills Boulevard. The phone he had answered was on his nightstand in his bedroom. When he hung up, he walked into the living room, which was furnished like a den, and sat down on the black leather couch to think. Suddenly the truth had to be faced. Until this time it had just been talk. He was nervous. He loved Lorene so very much, and now a piece of paper might take her away. He sat for a few minutes, and then he gathered his things and went downstairs to the lobby where the mailboxes lined one wall in an alcove. He was so very anxious to get the results and, at the same time, just as Lorene felt, he was frightened to find out. He reached in his pocket to get the mailbox key. He was so nervous that at first it seemed that the key didn't fit. When he finally opened the box, there it was. The letter had arrived. He took it out, relocked the box, and carried the official-looking letter back to his apartment. He was tempted to open it, but he refrained because he had promised Lorene they would read the letters together. *How will I feel if I find out that Lorene's father was my father too?* he questioned himself. He had thought about it before, but now that he was about to find out, the question seemed much more relevant. He put on a light cardigan and headed out the door to the garage in the building where his car was parked. *It won't take me long to drive from Queens to Long Island*, he thought. *I'll be there on time.*

Lorene had gone to the window dozens of times and watched as various cars drove by. This time a car parked. Ray was finally there. She ran to the front door and opened it wide, waiting for him to get out of his car, walk up the path, and greet her with a hug. As he entered he took an envelope out of his pocket, waved it, and said, "I got mine too."

"Come into the den. I left my letter there," she said. Then she asked, "Did you open your letter?"

"No, I waited to be with you. We should do this together."

Lorene seated herself on the couch, and Ray sat down in an armchair next to the couch.

"I am so nervous, Ray. I want to know what it says, and at the same time I don't want to know."

"I feel the same way. But we agreed to do this, so we have to see it through."

"You open them both and then give me the news," she said.

"Are you sure that's what you want? Shall I read them aloud?"

"No, read them to yourself. I'm too nervous. You can tell me what they say. Here's my letter," she said. She picked her letter up from the end table, walked to Ray, and handed it to him before sitting back down on the couch.

"I'll read mine first." He tore open the envelope and unfolded the sheet of paper.

Lorene watched Ray's expression for some indication of what the contents were, but she could not tell what he was thinking or whether the news was good or bad. When he finished reading his letter, he carefully refolded it and put it back in the envelope. Then he tore open her envelope, removed the paper, and read silently. He continued to remain expressionless. Finally, he folded her letter and returned it to its envelope. He took both the letters and reached out to hand them to her. She looked at him and said, "No, I don't want to see them." She stood up and walked over to him.

"Ray, before you say anything, before you tell me the results, I want you to know that no matter what the tests showed, it doesn't matter. I love you, I always have, and I always will. "

Ray got down on one knee in front of Lorene and asked, "Darling, will you marry me?"

Her answer came rapidly. "Nothing would make me happier." His question gave her the answer.

Ray took the two letters and in one motion ripped them in half and dropped them in the wastebasket. "Let's just file these," he said as he and Lorene embraced.

Questions for Book Club Discussion

1. How would this story have changed if it happened today?
2. Why do you think the author chose the quote *"Est modus in rebus"*?
3. Is this a good title for the book? How does it relate to the contents?
4. Was your interest sustained as you read the book?
5. What was more important—the plot or the characters?
6. What moral or ethical choices did the characters make?
7. Which character changed or evolved the most over the course of the story?
8. Do the characters seem real and believable?
9. What was the message the author wanted to convey?
10. Which character was the most sympathetic?

Commentary

During my lifetime, I have lived through several wars—World War II, the Korean War, and Vietnam, plus Iran and Iraq. I know that many lonely servicemen had romances with girls wherever they were stationed. "A girl in every port" was a sort of motto of the sailors.

Out of those love affairs, many children were born. Some were abandoned by the fathers, some were adopted by the fathers, and in many cases, the fathers were unknown.

I became interested in the lives of these wartime babies and speculated on what may have happened to them. Out of my speculations, the plot was born for *No Time to Regret*.

Carrying my plot further, I have thought about whether, in the future, DNA tests will be required each time a marriage license is issued. Since our lifestyles have changed so radically and adoptions have increased in frequency, many couples may not know anything of their backgrounds.

About the Author

Lynne List, PhD, is a retired Professor Emeritus who taught at the undergraduate and graduate levels after a career as a classroom, reading teacher and reading consultant.

She coauthored one college textbook and authored another herself. She has published numerous educational articles. In addition, she has been included in 13 "Who's Who" volumes. Her avocation is theater and bridge.

She wrote three plays one of which took first place in a new playwriting competition and had a successful staged reading in a professional theater. In addition, she acted in and directed many shows. Her second avocation is duplicate bridge; a game she loves and plays frequently. This is her first novel.

Printed in the United States
By Bookmasters